OPEN DISTANCE

MICHAEL VORHIS

DEDICATION

This book is dedicated to those people in my life who have encouraged the real living of it—initially my mother, spirited to the end, and my father, whose instruction on all things competitive and mechanical captured and held my imagination—and to siblings who either shared in adventures, or followed them vicariously, or admonished against them in ways that drove me onward. And I will never forget the brothers I chose, down through the years—the kindred spirits with whom I explored alien realms, taunted unnamed perils, and tasted unspeakable glories, for they learned alongside me that Life belongs to those who can't get enough of it.

CONTENTS

ACKNOWLEDGMENTS

I'd like to express a very special thanks to my wife Linh, my daughter Véronique, Bob and Liz Owen, fellow soaring pilots Alan Kenny and Don Burns, general aviation pilot and diver Gopal Ramachandran, Bernie and Dan, Vinita, Donna, Horace Johnson, author Will Chaffey, and my Father, for their varied and individually invaluable input toward my honing of this work.

CHAPTER ONE

This may be my last testament—at least, about what I'm going to say. Guess I'll say it now before I lose my nerve.

I'm sitting here, alone, calm sea. Incredibly deep here. The shear of the current is as light as I can remember it ever being. The ocean is truly our cradle, from long before our species existed until...I guess...the end of our days. It's so quiet. I haven't popped the hatch yet, but at some point I guess I will, and put an end to all of it.

Alone. In fact that's part of the theme of this whole story—my story. I realize I've been alone for a long time, bordering on forever, and now again. I don't know the point when I began to think I wasn't, but I guess it was only maybe an hour ago.

It's hard to think about death with a calm mind. I feel like sticking the flare gun in my mouth. I never figured that when I confronted the Reaper or took his twisted, thieving ass seriously that I'd do it carrying the ugly weight of shame.

In the time left I'll do my best to explain, to tell the whole tale. Not sure if my account is going to make sense...in sequence and all...being that I'm talking it into this thing, this voice recorder, straight out of my head. Might be enough charge in the power cell to get the whole thing out. I'll say now, to Jeannie and Karina, I love you both more than anything...you're all that's left that has ever given meaning to my life...and then it's probably best to start at the beginning.

CHAPTER TWO

I can't seem to get the Outer Banks Open out of my mind. I know that's not exactly the start of this story but it's so typical of how it's always gone. I'm talking about the last one—the one just last spring. Most of my team showed up for it, although it was not really a team meet. Marc didn't show, nor did Will because his pod had a leak, but Paul, Alan, Bob, Ted and Rick did. I don't think the Outer Banks ever did any team scoring or NAI team ranking stuff—but still we always help each other, share strategy, stuff like that. We have a good time with it. My team hails mostly from the Midwestern USA originally, Michigan and Illinois...eastern Missouri...me, Ohio...maybe it's that Midwest connection that gravitated us to each other...although the sport has pulled most of the guys to coastal towns here and there, where they can free-fly in the off-season. And I do fresh water, and travel, to accomplish the same thing.

People always point this out more than I ever did because I don't like to make it a bragging thing, but to be honest I was probably the one person most responsible for this bizarre sport getting organized and taking shape. Funny how a world-wide fascination can start with just one guy. I guess that says something about how amazing a thing it is, and maybe how much of a millennia-old longing it was for our species, to explore the forbidden habitats of our planet through various kinds of flight. But even so, how many of us get steered by Destiny to be that single focal point of something, across all of humanity and all of time? Yet that's how it fell out for me. Just dumb luck.

Like a lot of guys, I'd flown air in homemade fabric wing gliders as a teenager, making the things from kits in the beginning, and launching off the back hill, surviving my share of skinned knees and bonked heads...little by little learning to watch the wind directions and velocities so I could stay in the air for seconds, then minutes, then eventually much longer periods of time. Everybody who gets into that stuff yearns to be able to park the wing in upwardly deflected mechanical lift on some windward-facing hillside and just marvel at being motionless above ground with no visible support. Those modest little goals are great motivators, and I paid attention, and applied my analytical "figure out the details" nature, and learned well. So over time I came to know intuitively how airfoil attack angle and drag and span all affect efficiency. Must have built thirty different variations, and amazingly in all that experimentation never really got hurt. Much, anyway. I wasn't very supervised back then, and when you're young you think you're immortal. Wish I believed in immortality right now...but I guess that concept has always been a lie.

I got to where I could launch a hang glider of my own making in laminar wind and climb to several thousand feet all the time, when conditions were right anyway, and angle out here or there on some cross-country escapade—and not always downwind, either. None of this was unique to me, because others around the country and world were doing it too, although rarely were any of them as thoroughly self-taught. I was in a vacuum, and more than that, what made me so different was that in all that unbelievable accomplishment and hypnotically applied energy, I was pretending I was doing something else.

I read somewhere that Christopher Columbus, a man who may have made the greatest discovery in all of human history, went to his deathbed denying he'd done any such thing. He went mad insisting he'd found the westward route to the Orient, as had been his goal. Something like that. Total mind-losing focus. And in a similar way, amazingly I was blind to the heroism of daring to fly in the sky by force of will alone. Blind to it! Instead I imagined myself emulating my own heroes. They weren't aviators; their legacy and lore were much more ancient.

You see, as incredible as a man flying like a bird is, strangely my real fascination was for sailing ships—the ocean-going beauties of history and fable I'd read about as a kid, and seen magnificent drawings of, and that my Dad, a ship builder during the war, had described as I'd drifted off to sleep. The big square-riggers, the sloop-rigged, the frigate fleets and armadas, the intrepid prehistoric merchant vessels of the smaller seas, the Viking war ships, the whalers...and the pirates.

Ships probably lodged themselves in my mind because there was no water around where I grew up—we always yearn for the one thing we don't have. Since we didn't have anything bigger than creeks and quarries, I was naturally the most ardent sailing romantic ever born. My seafaring was all in books, in theories, and in eye-popping tales replaying each night inside my head. And strange as this sounds, in my late teen years I came to do amazing things in air without ever acknowledging how phenomenal they were. I was trying to do nothing more than emulate the daring exploits of men before the mast.

I'd actually climb in thermal lift to deadly altitudes and tack upwind like the schooners and ketches and yawls of old, imagining myself in the crow's nest or clutching the hemp of the aloft rigging, in reality just dangling from an unpowered fabric airfoil—nothing more than a glorified awning, or what motorized flyboys call flying lawn furniture—and sometimes going tens of miles. No training. No plan. No telling my dad later.

So I never really thought of myself as an aviator. I was a mariner plying an invisible Deep Blue. I did come to really understand airfoil efficiency in all its subtleties though; I was motivated, and flying was my outlet, the atmosphere above the Ohio farmlands my pretend-high-seas. I didn't have the right words for it all, but I'd fill in later with reading, and basically it all got into my blood and bones.

A lot of real aviators understand all that stuff too—angle of attack, chord profiles, drag, laminar flow...vortices...they get it all too, of course. And a few of them get the fact that gravity, not lift, is a glider's engine. Most of the people who will hear this tale I'm telling...that is, if anyone will...know that a glider can best be defined as a thing that slips off in some lateral direction through the air when gravity pulls straight down on it. How it does that is just detail; that's really all it is—a thing that slips off on an almost level path when pulled downward. It's just the shape of course, which is optimized for the thinness or heaviness of the fluid it's in—in this case thin. Air. It does go down a little, since gravity has hold of it. But it slides off wherever it's pointed a lot more. Just takes the path of least resistance, in its fall. Rest assured it will end up on the ground—gravity can be defied but can't be beaten. But if a glider can go ten feet straight for every foot it drops, that's a ten-to-one glide ratio. Then letting math and engineering nuts mess with subtleties of shape and elasticity can improve that a great deal.

At least, that's the simple way I conceptualized it, and still do.

But most soaring aviators spend their time hunting for lift, and so they think lift is the "engine" that powers their flight. Yes, it enables the exploits of the flight, all the stuff they put in the logbook. Sure. But the gliding itself—the slipping in a forward direction all the time instead of falling like a stone—is powered by gravity. And not every flyboy gets that. And I guess none of them ever got what one day hit me.

It was a day too strong to be in the air; even I, twenty-year-old Kid Solo, Kid Luck, Kid Immortal, Kid Stupid, knew when it was just way too strong. There's an old saying that pilots use when the sky is too rowdy; they say it to remind themselves that the better part of valor is discretion. Don't know who coined it first, but when we announce we're not going to fly, we explain the decision by reciting, "I'd rather be down here wishing I was up there, than up there wishing I was down here."

Well, that was such a day. Northeast wind, which meant a storm cell somewhere to the southeast. Don't want to share the sky with one of those. Already there were gust differentials of more than twenty miles per hour by the time I got home from a half day of classes –I was getting an engineering degree at Miami University in Oxford, this little southwest Ohio town up the road. Since flying was out of the question, I got out a big kite I'd been making for testing some airfoil shape modification or other. I tied a quarter-inch rope to it and lashed the free end to a heavy rusted one-bottom plow that had lain buried in the dirt on the back hill for a decade. I got the canopy in the air and let out rope until I'd positioned it about three hundred feet over the barn roof, where it could whip around but still stay aloft, free of the turbulence off the low row of trees just south of our house. I used a very small tail so it was marginally stable but would better show me its instabilities and its penetration capability into the wind.

And I watched it. For an hour. It worked alright, but that's not the point—I don't even remember what shape tweak I was testing at the time. The point is that I got bored watching it, and began to imagine it as a square-rigger's semi-triangular jib sail, only tethered by its rope to the rusting plow below instead of sideways to a ship's spar. The rope was the applied force against which the kite was "gliding," just like gravity was the applied force when I was hooked into the bigger "kite" I often flew around the valley.

So in this case—and I hope you can get this—the direction of the so-called tethering force was down the rope. For ship sails, the force is pointed sideways toward the spars and masts to which they're tied. For gliders, it's gravity, pointed straight down. Same idea, just different directions. So...I began to wonder...when we fly a gliding craft, why must we always be gliding against the same force, gravity, which always pulls straight down? Aren't there other forces in other directions we could glide against?

I thought about how a kite "glides" forward and upward when you run with the string on a still day, how your running applies a force along the string instead of straight down to the ground. Again, different from gravity's directly downward pull, but also exactly the same.

Well then, what other directions could a force pull? The seafaring romantic in me eventually got around to imagining buoyancy as a force. Could we glide against that? Why not? Hold a flat piece of wood at the bottom of a tub of water and let it go...it slides off to the side, back and forth, as it rises to the top. Isn't that gliding? It's coming up instead of going down, but otherwise it's the same idea—it slips sideways in some direction of least resistance when buoyancy pulls straight up on it.

I got so excited I left the kite tethered in the wind and ran inside to find some small flat piece of wood chip or other, which I feverishly whittled into a triangle shape...delta planform...and, as I recall, cutting my thumb in my haste. Didn't matter; I emptied the kitchen sink of dirty dishes and filled it with water, held the wood chip to the bottom, and let it go. Shape was wrong and it "dove" point-first to the surface after about a second, but I tried again with a wider nose angle, and again, and after a few tries and some care to not turbulate the water by yanking my hand out too fast, I got one of them to "glide" smoothly to the porcelain side wall of the basin without changing its rate of rise. I had made a tiny water glider.

Meanwhile the wind outside strengthened and switched, and the kite dove into the barn, and I don't remember if I ever got it flying again after that. Probably still have pieces of its frame somewhere, to this day. But I barely cared. Over the next few weeks I built two—what I called underwater kites—about three or four feet wide, tip to tip. I made them out of rigid closed cell foam. It was all intuitive, as I didn't know the math to model a more viscous fluid than air through which to "fly." And Reynolds Number theory was still way out of my league. I tried high and low aspect ratios, testing them in the swimming pool at school, initially getting in to launch them in waist-deep water by holding them down with my foot. Neither one worked perfectly and I made a third shape, cannibalizing the wider one to do so. Its shape was somewhere between those two first attempts, and it sorta worked. Part of the challenge was to shape it so it wouldn't turn, so that I could test the glide. But I saw that and added some small winglets to the tips, and a keel rudder, and that third one would glide from wherever I let it loose on the bottom to the side wall of the pool, and bump its nose there.

I was hooked, and dove into the fluid dynamics of it all. After another year of obsession, during which time I also began to figure out a "launch" procedure using a tow string from the water's surface—just like a kite string only the kite is going down through the water when the string is pulled, instead of up through the air—I got permission to do my undergrad thesis project on what I called the "Diving Aqua-Kite." Stupid name, but remember I was still a kid. Anyway I chose to make performance, including diving efficiency, max range, and time before surfacing, a major theme of the project. I guess I thought I needed some math to show for it if I was going to get a decent grade. I roped in a bunch of guys who had trouble coming up with project ideas of their own, to piggy-back onto mine in exchange for helping with calculations and carrying stuff around. Carl Maxwell, who became a buddy and later did a bit of flying with me, suggested we grab ourselves some notoriety by hyping it and holding an all-campus competition. We announced an Aqua-Kite day and talked the thing up. Got a bit of a turnout, actually. Maybe that was because engineering students are always suckers for a design-off, just like jocks are sure-shows for a track and field event. And this thing had it all over the usual egg drop and paper airplane challenges that most schools did. The School of Engineering endorsed it too—didn't take much to get the Dean to agree. Anyway we called it the "first annual," and it proved to be a good prophesy because it did happen the next couple of years too. Any student who wanted to— mostly from the Engineering department that first year—built kites to enter. Prize was something ridiculous like a couple of supreme pizzas, or a date with somebody who'd never agreed to any such thing. We launched everybody's aqua-kite in Winton Lake, which was right there next to campus, with a rowboat that had a tiny trolling motor. I heard that Purdue actually had a copycat event the next year. I was proud, but of course I secretly had bigger ideas, and was just warming up.

In the summer leading up to my senior year I built a big one. I got a part-time job at a river canoe livery where I didn't have to put in many hours, and spent the rest of my time designing and building. Took me weeks and weeks— hundreds of hours. The thing was crude by today's standards, in that it was made out of aluminum sheet material riveted and sealed to a frame of wood ribs. The wood was water-soaked and then bent to shape. It wasn't all that symmetrical, truth be told. It was hollow, something like a clamshell that flattened out left and right like wings, with a trailing tail like a stingray. I guess you could say I patterned it off the body shell of a crab, except for the addition of the stinger out the back. Needed that for static stability. As anyone would expect from a guy like me, I chose to build it like whaling boats had once been made—the bent wood ribs—and since I was guessing about the volume, flotation, and static trim, I installed thin pipes on the underside, from near the nose to all the way out the stinger, that I used as a kind of track on which I slid small weights, so that I could adjust the static weight distribution until it worked right. It was a long time later that I realized the tracks should have been on top so as not to spoil the inverse lift...but they did the job. And I put way too much hydro-stability in the shape of the control surfaces, but of course at the time I didn't know what the thing was going to need. Even so, ultimately these early experiments put me probably eighteen months ahead of anyone else in getting to the right understanding of static and dynamic balance. Anyway I sealed it with silicone sealer and a big fat gasket for the uncomfortably small gull-wing door, named it

"Aqua-pod" or just "The Pod," and like all those movies about reckless fictional vaccine inventors, I dispensed with intermediate proofs of concept and put it immediately to the ultimate human trial test.

We drove over to the quiet upper section of Cowan Lake, by Clarksville, just shy of the drowned trees. I climbed in and Carl towed me down. We'd done our best to estimate what my added weight would do to the buoyancy, and I stayed as still as I could in the center, because moving even a little in there seemed to pitch it up and down. Carl had borrowed a bigger outboard motor without actually telling the owner, and was arrested for it later that night and had to apologize and pay a bit of a fine. I paid it, of course, and neither of us regretted it, because the damned pod worked! First test proved it was way too tail heavy, so I slid the weights forward a good bit, and I leaned more forward inside, too. Then he towed me to six feet, then eight, then all the way to seventeen out in the main channel, where I hit the mud bottom. On the first two I stayed on tow and glided against buoyancy when Carl slowed and the rope went slack. The third time I released from the rope and took it as far as I could. I was able to glide over a hundred and ten feet before running out of depth. That's only about seven to one, maybe not quite, which is lousy in water, I know—lousy even in air for that matter—but it was incredible to us. When I bobbed to the surface and he spotted me, even with the pod still sealed I could hear him yelling his fool head off.

That first pod leaked, and was cramped as hell, but we did more that summer in the top twenty feet of depth. We moved our tests down-channel, nearer the spillway, where it was a little deeper. Flights weren't any longer than half a minute, but we got to almost ten to one. I cut a hole in the hull in front and sealed in a thick piece of clear acrylic sheet, for a window, which helped me go straighter and get a little bit of video in clearer water. The video footage proved to be good for promotion, to help me get donations to buy better materials and make better modifications. At some point a local paper picked up on it, then the evening news, and suddenly I had this incredible groundswell following. I wrote a design article for Popular Science and touched off a storm of questions, most of which I had to handle by writing a follow-up article. They paid me more for the second one, which helped. Canoe and kayak gear companies, sensing the next big water sport, began to extend consulting and partnership offers. And copycat designs, many of them with interesting variations, started to crop up, first in articles and sketches, then in kit form and custom "build to suit" plans. I took a short consulting job with a N.A.S.A. spin-off agency—funny how little my G.P.A mattered in all of this—and from composites and machined titanium we constructed three larger pods outfitted with oxygen and navigation instruments, each very expensive and each capable of glide ratios of nearly twenty six to one. Those guys knew their math. The prospect of an economical manned machine traveling great distances silently and invisibly seemed to appeal to military minds, but I was happy to oblige because I knew their injection of serious technology would soon spill directly into sport.

The public called it the "Ohio Hydro-wing" or the "Nolan Farragut Wing" for a while, after me, until it just got too big to be a parochial novelty anymore. Like hang gliding before it, it ignited a long-frustrated fascination in the human mind, this time for personal "everyman" deep water exploration. Pods started to be made by practically every composite gear outfit out there, and some entirely of metal by machine shops. And let me tell you, they sold like bass boats. Launching was so easy that anyone could do it, and at least in the absence of strong currents and obstructions, flying a pod was relatively safe. Shallow, anyway. Do nothing and you bob to the top. And unlike air space, there was little if any regulation underwater, so nobody needed a license; people could feel like they were flying and never fear a high speed impact, never go through a physical or even take a lesson...although self-proclaimed instructors became plentiful too. Suddenly everybody could live their Jules Verne-ish fantasies.

Also, with the use of a handful of pontoon boats that had TV monitors on board, and a few tethered underwater video cameras, it wasn't difficult to arrange for paying spectators. Even that gear, like turn point pylons with camera mounts and such, got easy to find in ready-made form after awhile. So, emulating existing nautical and aviation meets, event promoters began to define little sprint and duration regattas, area-contained obstacle courses, and then timed "cross-country" challenges, with complex tasks comprised of significant distances and turn points. "Aqua-Gliding," or "Deep Flying" as the pilots came to call it, was born...and its universally acknowledged inventor, yours truly, wasn't yet twenty four.

I made a good living just appearing at these things, and at sporting equipment trade shows. Of course I competed too, and helped to design meets. The comps were suddenly everywhere, like marathons and bike races and hot air balloon festivals. As with fun runs and volleyball tourneys before them, they started to become all the rage for signaling the start of the summer holiday season at every port town or lake resort area you could think of. Trendy. National and world associations formed, for sanctioning meets and officializing results. It was no great surprise that I did so well in the world and especially the national rankings, given that I was laying out the courses and that my idea of the perfect meet probably matched my own fortes. Not that I was trying to cheat, it's just that that's what happens. I got a bit of a name; gotta say I ate it up, too. There were other pilots who got pretty good as well, though, and among them eventually was Brian—the unlikely, uncomplicated, larger-than-life Brian Lunfer. In my mind he was a poser, a selfish irresponsible glory hound, a walking calamity, a low-class bully and a dishonest piece of crap.

CHAPTER THREE

I started to talk about last year's Outer Banks Open, but got sidetracked. Sorry...this is all out of order, I guess...that's how memory dumps sometimes are.

Like I said, the Outer Banks was an individual meet, but it was an "Open," so anyone could enter. There were classes of watercraft—"Formula Four," with length, beam, weight and buoyancy all strictly defined; "Unlimited," which really is only less limited, in that static buoyancy is the only parameter controlled; and "Recreational Class." We call that one "Cork Class." I guess we shouldn't laugh at the entry level crowd...they pay the lion's share of the bills for these meets...but those cheap things don't really even need an oxy system if you ask me— they bob to the top so quickly it doesn't matter. I doubt if anybody ever runs out of air in them.

Safe, because their pilots are the low-performance recreational, beginner, timid sort anyway, more there for the fun and the picnic on deck afterward. And when they float out, they give the rest of us a little more room to fly at depth.

A lot of what I'm saying into this thing is stuff all the other pilots know already. But even so I want to get it all out. My two daughters will want to know some day, if no one else. This is my chance to tell them.

Anyway...oh yeah, Outer Banks Open. Last spring. Paul, Alan, Bob, and Rick showed up. And Ted. They all flew Formula and I went Unlimited, as usual. I'd designed and built a really high performance glider by then, and had made mods to it that I didn't really explain to anyone, not even them. Mostly little turbulators on the leading edge, designed to extend laminar flow at low velocities, which is the speed range in which we spend most of our time. Everyone always laughed at my battered, seemingly low tech hulls, with their absence of new features like kick plates and automatic pitch trim...especially in the wake of the new sleek breed of machined and polished things, or those slick, anodized pods from Parcepp and Sonnenwende. They'd look at the pure perfection that shiny seamless manufacturing techniques allow on those high-dollar beauties, and then at the exposed Philips-head screws not quite tightened all the way in on my own prow, and they'd call me a "Grumman" or a "Mig," and have no end of fun with it. They all said that if I ever got proper gear I'd do more than just win meets—I'd set records no one could touch for a century.

But nobody ever measured the distance between those ugly protruding screw heads of mine—nobody ever did a little math and saw that they were carefully spaced in a progressive parabolic distribution as they marched outward from nose to wingtips. And so nobody ever guessed that they were turbulators, or that they could give me up to a half percent efficiency advantage at certain precise speeds. A half percent when working sinking convection to get deeper could buy me a minute or more over someone else plying the same current.

There, I've come clean on the screw heads; now everybody knows. Doesn't matter now. I guess I could have shared the secret with my team, especially in meets that scored team points...and with my clients, who paid me to develop my best ideas into their new lines. But you know, I wanted to win, to beat everybody. I had a reputation to uphold. Maybe I should have, though.

In these meets we get towed pretty deep. Maybe twelve to fourteen meters or so, before we release. Still, with a rise rate of ten or twenty feet per minute, we'd be back on top before they got the tow ropes out of the way. So just like soaring aircraft pilots, who go find rising air and work that lift to stay up and move on, we work sink. We find convection caused by thermal activity, which comes from the sun or in rare cases tiny geothermal vents heating the water in certain pinpoint areas. And we seek out the downwelling, the water that's going down. We circle in it, or ride it linearly when it's distributed that way—we stay in it and turn modest depths into truly dangerous ones. The deeper we go, the better our glide ratio gets and the further we can go on a bit of depth...because the better pods compress a bit and get less buoyant—even the metal ones. But that compression adds risk, too, and the hulls have to be able to withstand that. We've all seen movies of Second World War subs sinking too deep and their bolts and rivets shooting inward, like small cannonballs, from the force of the pressure. In truth if that kind of breach began at serious depth, the whole craft would instantly crumple into something that looked like a tight ball of aluminum foil with a crushed body somewhere inside it.

That's the biggest danger. We're not going to pop out of a perfectly good pod and get eaten by some sea creature, not at any depth anyway...although if something happens at shallow levels and we get the idea to swim out of trouble, we may have to give that some thought...and that brings me back to the Outer Banks Open, because that's exactly what happened. But in general the danger is depth, and all the depth-related respiratory stuff like the bends, narcosis, oxy poisoning...like releasing pod pressure too fast, or the drunken, deep rapture effect—they call it "Martini's Law" and say every atmosphere and a half of pressure is like another stiff drink—or being killed by too much oxygen, believe it or not.

But our pods are really well designed these days, the mainstream ones from the serious manufacturers anyway, with special air systems—we usually just say "air" but they're actually high-tech breathing mixtures, to be precise, and we now use re-breathers and O2 harvesters too. Good pods also have active EQ control, and pressure spread very evenly over arch-shaped hulls that can withstand a lot. At the point in time of last spring's Outer Banks, if you were flying the latest gear of the day, you could be at something like a hundred feet, where an open water diver would be feeling four atmospheres of pressure, but a pod would hold a lot of that out. It compresses less, so you'd only feel a fraction of that. It's not linear because there's always the one atmosphere base line, but most guys at ninety-some feet last spring would feel pressure like they were scuba diving at around forty five or fifty, give or take, depending on the make.

So in addition to slow computer-controlled pressure bleed-offs, a pod will also just plain hold some of the pressure out, like the big military subs do. And now, as of this past summer, there's the new Life Chamber, and some unbelievable new composite materials, which brings that pressure tolerance idea to a whole new level.

But none of that innovation has made things any safer. We've simply used the extra structural integrity to convince ourselves we can go deeper and further. We've traded away that extra safety margin in our thirst for more performance and more amazing exploits. We're always on that ragged edge of what we consider acceptable risk. Just like in hang gliding competition, now and then somebody doesn't come home, and no one knows exactly what happened. But we all want to win; we all want glory.

Glory. A cosmic voice that will never whisper my name again.

Outer Banks...yeah...but I'll clarify one more technical thing first, and then get on with the juicy bits. For anyone who may ever listen to this recording who's not a pilot, the point about depth is going to be important as you hear my whole tale—not only last spring's Outer Banks, but even more so what occurred here, today, at the Worlds. It affects what happened, and to whom, and why. The basic point is, pods don't hold back all the pressure. They oil-can just a little bit—they squeeze down some, under load. I guess they could be built to be more rigid, but it would add cost. It improves year by year, like the Life Chamber, but still everything is compressible at some depth.

Virtually all competition pods use a dual skin design—the so-called I-beam effect makes it strong for the weight. For thermal insulation there's some semi-stiff foam between the two thin concentric skins, a little bit like what they use for bicycle helmets. Closed cell stuff, so that it resists some crushing. But unlike helmets, for pods it has to be a little bit flexible so it won't break up when the deep squeeze begins, or in transit on a car-top rack.

The deep squeeze sounds horribly deadly, and even top pilots quake in fear of it. But I'll tell you...it's actually a way to cheat...or, let's step around that harsh word and say it's a way to gain an advantage, if you have the bollocks to mess with it. Pods have to have some minimum buoyancy, to keep things fair, and the foam layer gives some of that. Still, at depth it squishes just a little. The pod becomes less buoyant then. Scuba divers experience the same effect when their wetsuits squeeze thinner as they descend. With pods, getting less buoyant is like a hang glider in low gravity...the glide gets better. And since I designed my own pods, I always secretly tried to make my foam layers even more elastic than normal, even more compressible, because I like to go deep and get more advantage. Risky, but then I always wanted to win.

Accepting more and more deadly risk in the quest for immortality is like drinking more and more magical snake venom hoping to achieve eternal health. That has become clear to me today.

Anyway, last spring, at the Outer Banks Open, we towed down one by one. Unlimited Class goes first, so we can try to get out of the way of the Corks—same as with the starting order at marathons, where the seeded runners are up front so they don't have to fight their way through the crowd. Brian Lunfer towed down first at the Outer Banks, always putting on the bold front, always trying to be a big shot. Being first has its advantages, but most of us prefer to hear the radio chatter of the first few, so that we can get a bead on what conditions are like. It's a timed race to goal, and at some meets every pilot's clock starts the moment he or she submerges, so floundering around figuring out what the water is like or where the convection is happening can hurt your time. Anyway, last spring he went down before I even vaulted the rail of the tug to get into the water, and I thought he was gone.

In the water I'd lined up second to last in my class, and eventually it was time to go. The rest of my team was flying Formula Four class, and so they were on deck—uh, that is, up next. I hooked onto the tow rope and sealed my old pod; the flagman on the tug's stern stood poised in anticipation for a moment, awaiting my signal, then waved the green stripes, telling me it was happening. They gunned the big engines, the froth piled up on my bow, and I turned the nose down sharply with a swift elevator input on my control stick. I added a bit of weight shift too; my pod was marginally pitch stable and prone to skipping on the surface at higher tow speeds, and I'd usually compensate by leaning almost as far forward as I could inside, until it bit and the down-planing commenced.

I took it to about as low as I dared, based on the depth there. You don't want to tow into the bottom; on rare occasions guys have done that, and with the size of the tug engines what they are today, it's instant pod destruction if you do. And if the tow line release gets bent, you may be still attached, and you and your pod can get dragged like an anchor into and through whatever the bottom holds, usually broken and leaking like a sieve, until the tug up top realizes there's far too much jerking and line pressure, and cuts their engines and tries to retrieve you...with a diver, if you're not too deep, or some other way if you are. Towing mistakes are bad news. Luckily they're never ultra-deep incidents, because the tow line is only so long, and luckily pilots don't fly into the bottom very often. But it has happened a couple of times—sometimes the guy did it because things weren't quite as flat down there as he'd assumed, sometimes because the release jammed—maybe the pilot forgot to pre-flight the thing, and didn't leave enough time margin to hit the secondary...or didn't have a working secondary...and sometimes just because somebody was daydreaming or was stupid...like the Corks. That's why the meet organizers sound out everything in the area in advance, and they also short-line the Corks, to limit the chance of accidents.

Still, for the other classes, every pilot knows that staying on tow is the fastest way to get deep—way faster than snooping out sinking water and working it downward—so Unlimited and Formula pilots tend to stay on the tow rope as long as we dare. I think at that particular Outer Banks the bottom below the tug was about seventy five feet down, so I took it to about sixty and then released.

There are other ways to screw up your tow; you can get a lock-out if the line is attached in the wrong place, or if your heading deviates on tow. Guys have done that too—they've gotten out to the left or right and then spun, twisting the line up, like a huge fishing lure that's fouled in some way. In aviation that's death, but in Deep Flying it mostly scrambles the pilot's stomach until he pukes, and until the tug operator notices and cuts the line or the engine. Then the pod generally pops to the top, right-side-up or not. Basically we gotta try to stay in line with the tug. It's hard to do because you can't see it up there above you, but you can usually see the line if you have a bow window, which most of us do. I've gotten out to the side more than once, but I've always applied input right away and avoided the washing machine ride.

Anyway I think I released at about sixty feet. I remember waffling around here and there, and the water was working reasonably well. Wasn't going to be a world record day, but I was optimistic as I got into the groove. It's actually easier to win a meet when the convection isn't gangbusters; anybody can go fast on cannot-fail days, when the difference in times between the first five can often be measured in seconds. And sometimes an ignorant nobody will stumble onto the flight of his life on a day like that, maybe by crossing some unthinkably stupid reef area and still finding sink and getting away with it, and that's when there's an upset. But on days that need a fair amount of judgment and decision, experience counts for a lot more, and that's good for guys like me.

Anyway, this was a day that my seasoning should have paid off. I'd planned to angle toward deeper water, knowing that the extra distance I'd have to fly would easily be offset by the strength of convection I'd find out there, and by the better glide I'd get. The benefits are somewhere between linear and exponential, for every meter of depth you add. I'd worked out a chart at one point, for my glider only—and that's another reason why I never wanted to switch to some fancy new pod. I knew my own gear, and I knew my self-designed, self-built pod was more compressible. Others were safer, but mine won meets. Other comp pilots would ask me about that now and again, but nobody could prove anything. Unlimited Class buoyancy compliance tests are all done in shallow water. Some might call it cheating, given that at depth I was running with less buoyancy than anyone else, but I saw it as "compliance with the rule at the point where the rule is measured." That's all I needed to claim. It was an edge I'd planned, done the math for, and guarded jealously.

So...where was I? I was working my way toward the deeper stretch. Water was cloudy in places, and I remember somebody's wingtip just barely grazed me on my top surface. It happens, but you don't expect it if you've towed down last and the Formula and amateur lot aren't in the water yet. Pilots overtaking from behind are supposed to keep an eye out for each others' little red tail light, usually out at the tip of the stinger or on a wingtip's trailing edge, and not get so close. I grabbed the low frequency sonic to curse him. Going low-sonic instead of hydrophone is what we do when we want to be loud and local, but only pod-to-pod—keep it mano a mano. It's bass only, but we can all understand it, especially the words I used. I swore at him...and damned if it wasn't Lunfer who answered! He had an unmistakable pod profile, too, and when he came out in front I could see him on my screen, my electronic flat panel...and he knew it. His subsonic came back at me as a big deep "Yee Haaaaw" and a gravelly belly laugh, all in the throaty sound that travels through water, wood, titanium, and the portions of the frontal lobes that register rage.

I swore again and switched to my hydrophone, so that everyone else could hear too. We get lazy and call them "radios" sometimes, me included, since the sound goes to the surface, gets converted to radio frequency at the meet's nearest comm buoy, and is then re-transmitted as RF to the tug. The pods around us still hear the sonic part of course. "Lunfer, what the hell...?" I said into the mic. Told him to take some goddamn lessons, learn to steer. I knew everybody on the tug could hear it. He didn't answer, except to rock his pod back and forth, mocking how aviators salute each other, and then he shot off in a line that was roughly parallel to the coast.

I knew already that Lunfer...Brian...was no slouch as a pilot...not at that point, certainly. And I knew I wasn't going to let him rob me of a first place showing. As I said, it happens, even to rank amateurs sometimes, if they take huge chances and get away with it. He was more than capable of that kind of recklessness, too, plus the guy had some skills. If he won the day it would put him within a handful of points of catching me in the overall meet, and I needed this win. My pod was better, and I was better, and smarter...although he's not the dumb-ass he lets on to be. I made a snap decision, changed my flight plan, decided to forego my deep route, and followed him, figuring I could hang with him until we crossed the channel in the last leg, after which I'd use my better glide at depth to straight-line to goal without having to find additional sink—I wouldn't be losing as much depth per mile as he would. Basically I'd just shoot past and take the lead. Seemed doable...seemed best to not let him out of my sight.

Trying to follow a reckless fool is the best way I know to teach oneself the difference between winning on skill and winning by giving away your safety margin. You can sure make good time if you take unbelievable chances. The guy flirted with bobbing out and ending his run at every turn—it was no wonder he had the highest no-show-at-goal rate of any leading competitor. He was like the ball player who on every pitch swings for the fence that's behind the parking lot that's behind the center field wall. There was no middle ground—either he'd turn in an unbelievable time or he'd zero the day.

I had to admit that, judgment aside, he had his moments. The guy could work the lightest sink in the shallowest water of anybody I'd seen, and hanging on his tail took every bit of concentration I could muster. I was out of my league; none of my mainstay skills and tricks applied in this semi-shallow sunlit zone, and I was reduced to scratching for sink in every tiny shred of downwelling I stumbled into, just to keep from hitting the choppy wave-washed ceiling above. And every minute I got a little farther behind.

And he knew I was on his tail. We were alone in his zone; he'd suckered me into his zone.

CHAPTER FOUR

I remember being so focused on not hitting the surface that I ignored all other concerns. The embarrassment of bobbing to the top, especially if Lunfer was there and did not, would be something I'd never live down...and I couldn't bear to lose to someone I despised so...openly. I was cursing my stupidity for falling into his too-obvious, pathetic little ambush, and simultaneously wondering if I could get his flight disqualified because he'd collided with me...and also realizing how petty that would sound. All this was going through my head when, about eighty feet down and maybe thirty and change off the bottom, there was a horrible dull thud, and my pod suddenly spun sharply to the left, upended, and came to a complete stop.

I already knew, but with a scowl I darted a look at the display screen anyway, and then when I realized it had failed, confirmed with a glance out the window. Brian had lured me into a kelp forest. He must have known it was there, and that I'd be unaware and would not be paying attention to the screen, to the ghostings of the large vertical tree-like sentries looming silently, ominously, all around. Maybe this was his way of showing me he was better than me at something, but I saw it as a dangerous stunt and I hated him double for it. I'd now lose the meet, at the very least. A big fat zero for the day, which would drop my standing even below some of the amateurs. My left wingtip had impacted a stalk and had gotten hung up, maybe on one of the protruding screw heads, or on the outboard control surface linkage. I was dangling sideways, lower wingtip stuck on the kelp stalk, the rest of the pod floating upward from that hang point, which explained why my body was stuffed into the left corner of the cockpit.

Luckily I hadn't collided a knee into the hull's skin; I'd taken the impact instead on my spine, against a stiff wooden structural support. It hurt. And my shoulder had ripped out the battery cable, which meant that nothing, including screen, secondary air regulator, and comm transceivers, was going to work. I braced a foot against the control panel frame and an elbow on one of the pod's tensioned ribs, and righted myself in the tiny sideways-hanging craft, hoping to get a better view of the outside, and what part of the wing was hanging me up. If I could break free and level off instantly, and if the thing would still steer right, I might yet be able to find some sink and save this situation. It wasn't likely, but all I could think of was Lunfer gloating out there and then making some mistake of his own, and maybe getting hung up too, only to spot me gliding on by and leaving him there to rot while I won the meet.

Those hopes crumbled when some serious bouncing—in a rage, of course—failed to free the pod. It's not like you're hanging downward in something, where you could jump and stomp like a madman and cause tremendous downward impulses, to tear free. Instead you're dangling upward, like a cork tied to a string snagged on something below. You can leap and wiggle and cause your pod to bounce slightly downward, but then it always floats upward at the same graceful rate, and it's not exactly surging up with extreme force. At any rate, it certainly wasn't enough to tear me free of the kelp.

That meant I was going to have to swim out...which meant I'd have to get one last breath and then hold it while struggling to breach the hull, incur some instant rush of pressure when I broke through, then quickly and with bare hands tear a hole big enough to get out, and leave the pod, maybe never finding it again. I'd have to risk hypothermia and whatever other dangers were out there, like, I was thinking, stinging jellies or what-have-you, then make it eighty-odd feet to the top while blowing out what was left of my single breath...and somehow avoid the bends in all this—which meant doing an impossible five-minute-or-more decompression stop, now on a stale half-lungful, and I knew that wasn't going to happen...so the bends would be a near certainty. Then I'd need to swim who knows how far to shore in whatever condition I was in by then...maybe be faced with climbing some crumbling cliff of mud or something...and if I somehow survived all that, probably walk miles exhausted and shivering until I could find help. All that alone; not even the James Bond writers come near all that. The troops weren't coming...my team wouldn't realize I was in trouble because I was way ahead of them, and off my expected course too, so even if they did figure it all out, they'd never know where to look. And nobody on the tug would think it odd that I wasn't transmitting. Everyone knew I didn't like to jabber on the subsonic or the hydrophone; I was old school, you see, and always used to brag about keeping it minimalist.

I climbed up to the other side of the cockpit and while balancing there did my best to re-attach the battery cable, but it had pulled right out of the termination fitting. I'd need a cable cutter and crimper to fix it, and of course didn't have that stuff on me. My battery terminals weren't posts; they were deeply recessed. No way to even hold the ripped-out cable temporarily against the terminal. So radio—that is, hydrophone—wasn't an option, nor of course was low sonic, and I swore a string of oaths, and looked again across to the little acrylic window where it was fogging up, and to the tall vertical shapes outside.

A lot of people may not think a plant that needs sunlight for photosynthesis can be found that deep, but I can tell you kelp can thrive there. Things change in the ocean, just like on land; things are always evolving. When predator species like crabs and lobsters deplete, like due to harvesting pressure, and can no longer keep their own prey in check, balances are disrupted and the whole ecosystem goes into some different phase, marked by greater abundance of other things...like sea urchins, when there aren't enough enemies to eat them. Urchins can chew kelp down to nothing in large areas. People get used to not seeing kelp and they assume the water's naturally wrong for it, but there are still pockets where the crabs aren't taken, where it's too exposed or for whatever reason the crab-and-lobster-pot guys go elsewhere. Kelp hangs on in such places and adapts as needed. It's there, believe me; it cost me that meet last spring and came very close to costing me my life. I knew Lunfer knew it was there—the water was very clear there, and tides fluctuate enough that sunlight penetrates to those levels at certain times of some days. I was sure he would have scouted in advance. I knew he knew it.

I'd already discounted the likelihood of getting out through the hatch—opening it cleanly at that depth, with that pressure, would take more force than I'd be able to apply. I'd have to attack the hull at a corner of the cockpit where it was weakest..I was thinking the low wingtip, where I could push with my feet. If I broke it open but not cleanly enough to get out fast, I could easily drown inside. A pretty little self-made, gracefully shaped pod of a coffin. Even if I made it, the water rushing into the cockpit would ruin thousands of dollars of instrumentation. And the worst part I didn't even know, until I took another long, careful look out the tiny window. It was now completely fogged up from all my exertion, and when I wiped it clean I saw a shadow, and it was big. My idiotic thrashing had attracted a tiger shark.

I watched carefully, suddenly very still and quiet, but inwardly kicking myself all the harder. I didn't see it for a couple of minutes, and tried to convince myself it had just cruised on by, but then the shadow returned. Its silhouette was unmistakable, and the thing was not a juvenile. It kept making passes, each time a little closer and a little more erratically. Cats have their twitching tails, dogs their curling lips and laid-back ears, bears their intense direct stare; these are the signs of agitation and aggression in the wild. I can't read the attitude and posture of sharks, but there's no question they have them, and those who share their habitat certainly can. I saw that every time the thing made a fly-by, the kelp forest community would be suddenly vacated by other forms of life. They could tell, and that told me: This was a predator in search of a meal.

It was all very bad. Transmitters down, oxygen limited, I didn't know if I could get out, and I didn't know how long I'd last if I did. Imagining what it must be like to have a cold-eyed, malevolent predator chew off your legs and then frenzy on your torso while your eyes watch, I have to say that meet scoring and revenge on Lunfer began to fade in importance in my mind. I had two little girls I swore I'd never abandon. I had to get out, but at the moment it would be suicide. I couldn't even go back to bouncing to try to free up the pod, because thrashing was sure to keep that killing machine close by. The only thing I could do right then was to wait. I sat there in the sideways-hanging pod, one leg braced against the control console and one arm cramping where I gripped the edge of an oak floor rib. In a feeble attempt to find some kind of calming salvation, my terror-stricken mind turned to my wife.

CHAPTER FIVE

It's not often a man can say a broken leg is the best thing that ever happened to him. It wasn't my leg of course. I was near the end of my senior year at Miami U and had been admitted to the hospital there in Oxford, for being stupid. That's really what it was, although the paperwork was more kind—they weren't threatening to remove frontal brain lobes or anything. I'd flown a bit too deep in an early, flimsy, self-made pod that was far too weak to handle even those modest pressures, and the thing had buckled and crushed on me. It was only something like forty feet, but that pod had been tossed together out of bargain basement fiberglass in a day and a night, long before I knew how to mix epoxy or lay up composite laminates that could handle much of a load.

I'd been able to wiggle out with no big problem, but like an idiot forgot to exhale as I rose to the top. It had been a practice run before one of the early meets, or let's say a test run for that pod, and I was holding a watertight bladder containing a notebook and some other gear, and the thing was full of air. I bobbed up like a cork, holding onto it, and as the air in my lungs expanded during my ascent, it did a little rupturing of my lung tissue. Nothing serious, because I remembered and managed to blow some bubbles toward the end of the rise, but I sneezed a little red stuff after I got back on shore, and they took me in to make sure I was going to be okay. They also wanted to check on whether I had the bends, but it turned out I never really got any of the other usual symptoms. Actually, like I said, I hadn't been all that deep to begin with, or been down that long.

It was a wakeup call on several fronts, but that's not why I call it the best of fortunes. I was sitting in the hospital waiting area on the sofa when they wheeled her past. The TV was bigger out there in the hall, and they'd given me a roommate who had been in a motorcycle accident and needed his sleep, so I was out there with the families who were watching mindless game shows while waiting to see their favorite patients.

Adrienne's smile was the only thing bigger than her leg cast. She might have been on pain killers—probably was. But from the moment I saw her, I was the one who needed them. I noted the room they admitted her to, which was a double room, same as mine. I waited for her huge twenty-four-member family entourage to leave hours later...aunts and uncles and cousins and such...including a guy about my age who looked like a fast-living Romeo of some kind, but who left before the family did, so I gathered he was not going to be serious competition...and then after they all finally disappeared, I walked quietly in when the nurse ducked out, and sat down on the chair next to the other still-empty patient bed.

It took her a few moments to realize I was gazing at her, and then another minute or so to stop pretending she didn't know. But she was a rare beauty in that she wasn't rude, arrogant, timid, or bent on stroking her own ego at a stranger's expense. And she was above trying to prove her capacity for the pitiful bullying they love to call 'assertiveness.' In other words, she was happy to be genuine. Before long she tossed me a pleasant comment out of courtesy...and maybe as a small but gracious reward for my assuming she was worthy of a little extra attention.

"You're not the one who escaped from the iron lung, I hope," she said with a little chuckle.

I responded with something stupid like, "Is that what that thing was? All those blinking lights...so you mean...I haven't gone into the future after all?"

"How does one get out of those things without help?" she asked, switching gears but continuing the playfulness. "Is there a little back screen door or something?"

"I really couldn't say how most people do it," I replied after some faux thought. "Believe I was just lucky; I flexed this one tiny little muscle here..." I indicated a precise point on the back of one shoulder..."and kaboom. Big smoking hunks of steel everywhere. It's uncanny, really."

She pursed her lips and nodded, then asked whether they often let unstable patients wander the halls at will; I admitted that the tough part had been slipping past the FBI anti-terrorist guys posted outside my door. From there the nonsense just kinda flowed. I guess it's a bit of a relief to be talking about it now—guess I've kept it bottled up the last few years. The conversation went something like, um...with her saying something like, "So, are you lost then?"

"All my life, until now." I was being charming, you see.

"And now you're done with all that."

"Yep."

"All that irresponsibility...those childish, masculine ways...." I think that's how she put it.

"Oh, quite."

"So, what now, then?" I remember she was smiling in such a mischievous way. All I could think of was:

"I could start by signing your cast. It's fitting that a future begin with a signature."

"Commitment?"

"Commitment," I agreed. "Kinda."

I heard a chuckle escape, but she managed to stay in character.

"So...the cast," I repeated. "I think I see a spot open there somewhere. Between toes eleven and thirteen."

"How do I know you're not just a leg plaster groper on the loose?"

"I would never."

"Why not?" She feigned indignation.

"Every man is born what he is," I said. "I'm more of a groper of body casts. I'm true to that, uh, higher, calling."

It was crass, and more than a little bold, but faint hearts don't win fair maidens. And she tossed her head back and laughed out loud, and that long, loose, slightly disheveled brown hair was like wild ponies on the prairie.

Guess I'm kinda deviating from the story here. I don't much care. That's what happens when Death floats onto your view screen.

So...I was discharged from the hospital that afternoon—they only found a bit of an elevated pulse, and I attributed that to having met Adrienne. I dragged my feet deliberately in trying to arrange for a ride home, because I wanted to run into her accidentally in the lobby. Turns out they kept her an extra day, and I loitered for almost three hours until a nurse basically chased me out. I went home in a cab and drove back the next day in time to see her being wheeled through the hall in front of the waiting area. Destiny, that kind of timing. I was sure of it.

I remember standing off to the side, but she spotted me and called out, with her parents there and everything. She kidded that I'd never given her my autograph on the plaster, and I ran and got a pen, nearly knocking over a very angry orderly in the process, and wrote a big flowing John Hancock that stomped on two other sigs and was spelled an awful lot like a telephone number.

"Ooooo, I like a man who can Carpe the Diem," she smiled, and then her dad said something about not paying for her classical education so she could use Latin to flirt with boys, and added a hint of a warning lest I get it in my mind to carpe anything at all, and then he excused them all with an obligatory scowl followed by a glimmer of a wink to me, and they were gone.

And she did call. None of this cowardly gamesmanship nonsense like waiting some minimum number of days to be suitably aloof, either. She was better than that. She called me that very evening and we had a nice comical conversation about a nurse who had been stumping around her hospital room the night before like a quarter horse, and about the young buxom one who I swore had pinched me when I was on the table. Of course she accused me of making that up.

Over the next few months I got next to no water-glider flying in, partly because I wasn't supposed to subject myself to pressures for a good long while, and partly because I had discovered movies, and dinners at places that had tablecloths, and phone conversations...and love. I became the ultimate chivalrous provider of diversion and companionship while her leg healed, and she absolutely ate it up. In truth I was the guy she'd been looking for all her life, what with my intelligence, overall honesty, respect for her, and my reckless confidence in my own unfailing immortality. And...while this is the kiss of death for cheaper girls, it was like gold with her: Even her father took to me. I think secretly he couldn't stand that slick-haired narcissistic dude I'd seen among them at the hospital; in fact she never said much about the guy other than that his name was Jeremy and that he was brash and a loser. But I gathered he'd been somehow introduced to her through a friend's friend, and she'd felt compelled to go along with it. She'd known him only a very short while; he'd had a hand in causing her accident, too—speedboat thing, and he didn't know what the hell he was doing. She paid the price, not him. Of course he never apologized. You know the type—the world revolves around his right to take what he wants. The guy had the good sense, or more probably the cowardice, to not call or drop by again. Not that he would have caused me any problems either way; I think it was clear that for decency, brains, guts and class, he wasn't anywhere in my league.

Posers always pose for a reason. If they had quality, they wouldn't need to pose.

Adrienne and I were inseparable through the following autumn and Christmas season—I audited a graduate class just for the hell of it, and even took my holiday dinners with her family. There wasn't anything happening with what was left of mine anyway, and for once I didn't care. She was finishing up grad school that year, and already had a couple of offers lined up. Journalism...and she had the insights for it, despite her tender years. She was an artist with words and ideas, and maybe that's why we got along so well...me creative technically, her with her perceptive window on the human condition. Her dad and I had a good thing going too, as I said, which was something I missed at that time because of the loss of my father. Adrienne and I would sit on their porch while Antoine asked me all kinds of questions about flying, both air and water varieties, and I knew he admired my guts and was living a long-nurtured, secret fascination for adventure through me. He was a dad, but still a guy, and still young in his own mind. Her mom would play the hospitable hostess with lemonade or warm coffee or whatever the day called for, and with occasional little conversations of her own that she'd use to show me the family cared about me and welcomed me into their world. They were gracious in a way I admired, craved, and loved. Sometimes on warm nights when the front porch scene got late, as soon as the old man would excuse himself to turn in, Adrienne would move over to lean on me or sit on my knees, knowing it scared the hell out of me to think her dad might come back outside and catch us. But he never did; the twinkle in his eye as he went inside said that he knew youth. He'd been me long before, and had landed the same kind of classy girl when his turn had come around, and still had the gift of perfect timing. The minute he'd leave us alone Adrienne would kiss me and giggle while I looked over my shoulder, and now and then one thing would lead to another.

For a guy who has kited himself aloft in pre-storm winds and flown to serious depths in the open ocean, this might sound like a strange thing to say, but in early spring of that year I took the biggest chance of my life. I proposed. We were walking a ridge trail near the Hocking River valley in southeastern Ohio, a pretty little place with gurgling creeks and bluffs and wildflowers just beginning to peek out of what was left of the snow. I found a patch of ice, not wanting to sink into either wet slush or moist earth, and got down on one knee and popped the question. As I was hardly made of money, instead of something with a diamond stuck to it I had a steel ring I'd wrenched off a nautical shackle, hoping it would bring a smile. It did. She laughed and pulled me to my feet, and gave me the longest, tightest hug you can imagine, and then kissed me...and said no! And it didn't even bother me, because I knew at once what she meant—she meant yes, but only when the time was right. For now she wanted to enjoy where we were right then, exploring each other and building an increasingly deeper love.

And anyway I'd asked really only as a statement, not as a request—I'd done it to let her know how smitten I was. And she adored me for that. And I'd gotten the answer I'd hoped for after all, just not in the usual words.

I miss her right now. I miss my daughters, right now sleeping at Adrienne's parents' home. They don't know yet what has happened here. I wonder if they could ever understand; I wonder if they could ever know how much I love them right now, and their mother, out here in this tiny pod, in the blackness.

Adrienne and I were married a little over a half year later. Her dad gave us a beautiful send-off...or launch, in my lingo...whatever you want to call it. Almost everyone there was from her family and circle of friends. My best flying buddies showed up of course, and a few others I knew from the aqua-pod world showed up. Brian actually showed up, which I didn't expect. Jeans, but a collar shirt and a tie, which I believe must have been loaned to him in the back room by one of her uncles. He said very little. He knew I didn't want him there at all.

She and I moved into a little apartment, and made such a cozy home of it. She spared me the indignity of draping everything in pink flowers or teddy bears, and I really liked the quiet, domestic life. Such a contrast for me, and contrast is always appealing. I had a decent day job, and on the side continued consulting for companies, designing pods, sometimes giving promotional tours around the region and such, but mostly doing new concept development and some testing. Adrienne took a job writing for a publishing house that put out several different kinds of magazines, some gardening, some psychology, some political. They were based out of Chicago but had a nice editorial office in Cincinnati, where we lived. Adrienne loved the diversity and depth of the projects they gave her, and had the additional advantage of working with some seasoned old geezers, from whom she learned a lot. They'd been around but hadn't lost all that much of their passion for new angles, and they, in turn, fed off her freshness. As a team they all put out some really clever stuff. Now and then she'd get a by-line on an article mentioned on the cover, and she felt she was moving up in the journalism world.

I began to go to meets again, although only the biggest, and only about five or so a year. The "on the road every weekend" thing wasn't as appealing as it had once been, and I realized that all the action I'd sought in the old days had filled a void that was now nicely filled by my lovely wife and the life we were building. In the middle of the second year, she announced that we were going to be parents.

Jeannie was born two winters after the wedding. What a little ray of light she was. Karina too, who followed her sister by a bit over a year and a half. They're each different, but they know they're inseparable. Jeannie is the leader, being older and having the confidence she does. She writes, like her mother, and paints like Rembrandt, and combines every kind of intelligence there is, except maybe dolphin-like sonar. She might actually have that too. Can't hold a tune to save her life though. And little Karina will sit at a distance and melt you with huge eyes and the hint of a smile, and you just wonder what on earth she's thinking.

They need their mother. Nothing can be done about that now. And they need me, because I'm the only one left who knows what the four of us were like together. They need Family. How I've let them down, before, and now again today.

CHAPTER SIX

It's so deep here. Current hasn't gotten any stronger...not that I can tell, anyway. I still haven't popped the hatch. Don't want to face the reality of what has happened, I guess. Don't want to open this little cocoon, this little womb I'm in, and let in the truth, the finality, and Death's shadow.

I continue to just drift like any other piece of flotsam enveloped by the deep and mighty sea.

I guess I'll go on with this monolog awhile longer...battery seems to be holding up, and there's still a lot to get out...and this will be my one shot at it. I hope my daughters will understand some day.

Outer Banks Open...why can't I seem to finish that story? It's nothing compared to what has happened today, although at the time I thought it was the height of intrigue and peril. Okay, so let me just wrap it up, and you may get a picture of how I came to think of Brian Lunfer like I did. Of course the Outer Banks was just the cake's icing at the time; he'd already done far worse than that to me by then.

I had no doubt he'd forced me into that kelp bed. Why else would he cut across there? Lured me in, knowing I'd be caught unaware. It's the kind of thing you just don't do, no matter what the competitive stakes. We're all rivals, sure, but real deadly risk is another thing again. Kinda like football players who try to permanently injure other players, who lack the empathy to realize that the guy they're trying to demolish is just themselves in a different jersey. Or maybe they don't lack it—maybe it's a form of self hate.

Strange that I never gave that possibility any thought regarding Lunfer until just now, as I said it.

The fact that he'd more lured me than forced me into the danger zone was a fine point I didn't want to consider relevant. He was reckless, that was the point. Putting himself in danger didn't give him the right to put me into it. Or to leave me there. I was a dad. Of course I was sure he was gloating over the anguish I'd feel about that, as I died.

I found out later that about two hours before we'd launched the Unlimited Class, Brian had been seen snorkeling near where the pods were tethered to the tug. Rick told me. He'd seen Lunfer near my pod, acting like he'd gotten his shoulder scraped or snagged on the protruding screws along my glider's leading edge. He'd lingered there, fingering the screw heads, inspecting them. Now, Rick wrote it off to the same kind of curiosity any competition pilot might have when he saw what looked like shoddy workmanship of a top pilot's gear. But when I heard it, I was sure Lunfer had been imagining how to put me out of commission permanently. Snorkeling?! Come on, nobody snorkels at these meets. That's what I'd told Rick. And I decided that Lunfer had pictured how he might be able to get me snagged on something...like kelp. I told my team that later; they all thought I was imagining things, saying Brian couldn't possibly have put such a devious plan together in such a short period of time, including scouting the kelp beds and all, and that he was just looking to discover my edge...or was truly fish-gazing, like the simpleton he was. But I knew better.

I knew because there had been hostile words shortly before the launch window had opened. He'd approached me at the tug's rail, in that boastful, swaggering manner everyone else thought was so cute.

"Duuuuuuude!" How original.

"What?" I'd responded, hoping to end the conversation before it began.

"Sun's peekin' through," he'd said, cocking a disheveled head, raising a single eyebrow, gazing quizzically at the morning mist above our heads. All designed to be disarming while he sought to apply his shifty nature toward messing with my mind. "A good day to die."

I knew he'd used that line ever since the day Dustin Hoffman's classic "Little Big Man" film had hit late night TV. Still, it was suspicious he'd use it then, there.

"Sun is peeking through, Brian," I'd said. "You're quite the genius." It was pretty caustic, but there was already quite a bit of history between us by then. My disdain for him was no secret; I felt no need to disguise it. That's what a guy gets for getting into my space and into my face, I thought. I'd thought that all my life, in fact.

"Dude," he said with a scowl, "jus'...wishin' you well."

I stared at him for the barest split second, but didn't respond, instead turning back to scanning the water's surface, back to getting my head into my flight. I could hear his feet shuffling behind me for a full minute, making noise, making sure I couldn't pretend that I didn't know he was there. I didn't care.

Finally he said, "Hope ya get the flight o' yer life." Then he was gone. At the time the significance of that remark didn't register with me, but hours later, as I hung sideways at eighty feet with air running low and a carnivore waiting to feast on me the moment I popped out of my shell, you can bet it came back. And I knew Brian had planned to put me at serious risk.

He'd been trailing my totals by only a handful of points in the meet, which was one of the key meets of the season. That's all the proof I needed to realize how much it meant to the guy to beat me. Not that he hadn't beaten my life down to nothing by that time already, but...well, I'll...get into that later. Suffice it to say that my flying supremacy and my constant hinting at his stupidity were enough that I knew he was capable of almost anything. It might almost sound...I mean, my accusing him...but you see I had already hated him for a long time by then.

Anyway, there I was at eighty feet.

The race had already lasted more than an hour and a half, but the air...uh, breathing mixture...gauge was still in the green when I'd gotten snagged. I'd wasted far too much time agonizing about zeroing the round for the day and imagining how I'd get even with Lunfer. And of course waiting out the shark. What kind of attention span do they have? Are they smart enough to know there's a living thing in a big metal crab shell? Would it find something else to chase and eat? What the hell had Lunfer been thinking, and how could he plan such a thing? He was notoriously reckless and could just claim he didn't know, or didn't expect the worst, and they'd all believe him—everyone at my memorial service... everyone would be in attendance but me. They'd all buy it; but it's no excuse, and I didn't.

Here I was wasting time blaming him again, instead of saving my kids' dad's life.

Should I wait? For how long? Should I expect some kind of help to arrive? Lunfer would surely know something was wrong when I didn't show up at goal...no one expected the meet's top seed to fail to complete the day's task. They'd certainly know something was very wrong when I couldn't be found at all.

There were protocols for this sort of thing—they were only loosely followed for beginners, because the odds were that a missing novice pilot was just bobbing out there somewhere with a cheap second-hand transmitter that had no range. The sea was always littered with amateur pods for hours after these meets, until they went around scooping them up. But Unlimited Class pilots who went to serious depths and flew for serious mileage were supposed to be kept track of.

Even so, they knew how competitive I was and might assume that I'd accidentally floated out and was just sitting somewhere, drifting and pissed off. Even if they did get concerned, how would anyone know where to begin to look? Without hydrophone or low sonic or transponder signals guiding them, about all they could do would be to motor along the main course line looking for a guy sitting on his floating pod on the surface. Or for wreckage. They found Barney Sterlin that way once, off Sicily's eastern coast. They found that Galveston pilot, Doug Haller, too, but not his pod, and he was dead.

Lunfer had to know the most likely places for me to be found, but as reckless as he was, he wouldn't have noticed exactly where he'd lost me. And wouldn't have cared...or worse. I reasoned that he'd have just flown through as fast as he could to win the round, and then he'd be celebrating for a couple of hours with anyone who'd congratulate him and buy him drinks. No one would even know I'd been flying his same path; they'd all be looking along the deeper routes I'd normally have taken. Such an ass I'd been, to follow Lunfer—such an ass he was, to have suckered me in.

I wiped the fog off the window again, and looked out. The shark's shadow was still there. The fact that it hadn't spooked yet made it clear there were no boats churning up the surface above.

I sat and watched; it would disappear for awhile, tempting me to take a chance, only to drift in spookily again from high on the left side. It was flying a pattern, maximizing coverage while minimizing distance to a potential target. I had to assume it had decided where the thrashing had been coming from and that something was trapped there that didn't want to be eaten. Minutes seemed like weeks. My only movements became furtive glances from upper left to central right at the window, and then across to the air meter. I got to know what it feels like to be the worm on the hook.

Some time later...I don't know how long, but the air was real low by then, and I was minutes away from being forced into trying to exit the pod...a thud and a scraping sound...and it sounded metallic. Something had touched my glider! Something that sounded like metal had dragged momentarily across my hull. Some bit of flotsam trailing a steel cable? A fishing net or crab pot line? Someone's anchor? I held my breath, hoping for...I didn't know what. There, again...was that it, or something else? I vacillated between hope, doubt, and dread, waiting there with breath held. About five minutes later I heard it a third time! Didn't know what it was, but suddenly I could feel the pod tilting just a little. It started to change position, then went limp again, then half a minute later began to level upside down, until I was upended onto my back on its ceiling, balancing myself with a hand and an elbow across wooden ribs, like trying to stay on floor joists in an attic.

Whatever it was, I knew now it wasn't likely to be some accidental collision of debris. Someone or something was up there, and by chance or otherwise, had made physical contact, and had snagged against the pod. The shark problem could be gone at this point, I hoped; a lone hungry hunter like that might have spooked due to the sharp mechanical impact noises, and moved on. My mind was ticking off the various dangers one by one from a mental clipboard, you see; if the shark was gone, then one down and several to go. In my mind I flipped the toothy carnivore the finger, but I still had the breathable air problem, I was still hung up, and I was still way out there and way down there. And this new development was sure to be a freak accident, so my situation was still probably unknown to the rest of the world, other than to Lunfer.

The tilting became a sort of bucking, like something was surging in wild jerks. Could be tidal surge on some big drifting snag, I thought. At some point one of the pod's wooden floor ribs groaned and cracked, caused by grossly uneven tension from whatever had caught onto me. Pods are pretty strong as long as even pressure is applied all around, even my homemade thing; but they're not meant to be jerked violently by stuff. Where the wooden rib was no longer bracing, the hull skin tore open slightly in the wingtip corner. Water began to gush through the tear next to the seam. What pressure the pod had been holding out now suddenly equalized, and I was hit without warning by the full brunt of three and a half atmospheres of pressure, instead of the two and a half or so that I'd been subjected to with the thing intact. A sudden surge like that is pretty painful, not to mention the permanent damage it can do to eardrums. Desperately I sought to equalize, one hand on my nose, one still trying to stabilize myself on the rest of the ribs.

The cracked rib snapped outright, pointing inward, and the hull tear widened. At almost the same time I felt weightless for a split instant, which meant the pod had ripped free of the kelp. I caught a glimpse of the shades of green-grey beginning to change to lighter hues through the small bow window, meaning I was either rising, or turning, or both. And I wanted to tell myself I could feel the pressure changing in my ears, relieving that new pain.

I still kept my faculties through all this—I was a pretty seasoned thrill seeker, as are we all I guess. I knew that if the water didn't fill the pod first, I stood a chance of bobbing to the surface. That would solve the most imminent and deadly of my problems, and leave me to deal with the probable later onset of the bends, since my active pressure equalization system had gone off when I lost battery power...and wouldn't have done a damn thing with a breached hull anyway. I wasn't using any kind of well honed breathing mixture last spring...not like I used today for the Worlds...so gas bubbles were liable to lodge in my capillaries or joints. As serious as that was, it would be a later concern, and for the moment, if whatever had snagged me was some unmanned thing, a drifting telephone pole or something, it would leave me to figure out how to get to shore.

And how to go about setting things right.

In my excitement and with one hand still busy trying to equalize pressure in my ears, as the pod slowly began to surface I lost my balance. It spun as it rose, and dumped me against one bulkhead and then the floor, and I tried to compensate by whipping my leg out to the side. I succeeded only in impaling my calf muscle on the sword-like splintered floor rib! Went completely through, somewhat above the Achilles, protruding out the other side by a couple of inches. I howled like a little kid, and my pent-up rage added itself in. Skewered like that, I couldn't roll as the pod rolled, and I got to a point where my head was forced to stay down near the bottom of the control console. Water was seeping in badly, making it hard to keep my nose and mouth above the bloody red mess. What was taking so long with the damned surfacing?! So close to salvation, and now this...as I yelled in renewed fear and rage, the foul expletive came out sounding like Lunfer's name.

I did somehow manage to keep my head above water, or I wouldn't be here telling this now. The pressure change became unmistakable, and thankfully the seepage slowed down. I was pretty sure I'd surfaced. Whatever had hit my pod was still a big unknown. Again, could have been something like a hulking piece of loose waterlogged timber, drifting in the tidal surge by some unbelievable stroke of luck, maybe hovering near me just out of sight for an hour or more before accidentally plunging into my side or getting some trailing steel cables hung up. Or maybe an old fishing net, or a chain of a buoy that had broken loose. I just didn't know. Luckily whatever it was hadn't damaged the hatch. I was still likely to sink, by the looks of it—still needed to get out. I took a deep breath, gritted my teeth, and ripped my leg off the spear-shaped wooden splinter. The pain was horrible in that instant, but dulled amazingly quickly in the cold water. Ignoring it as best I could, and trying not to think about loss of blood or long swims trailing a stream of red juice out behind me, I checked that the hatch was pointed roughly upward, popped the latches, raised it, and stuck my head out.

The first thing I appreciated was the air. It was the world's promise to me that I was still alive. Since my head and shoulders had come out of the hatch facing land, I also immediately saw that I was only about a kilometer, actually less, from shore. Kelp everywhere, but I'd most likely be able to swim through it, even with a pierced leg...unless the shark or its buddies were cruising within that stretch. A high bluff tumbled from slanted hills into the sea, and continued steeply downward below the surface, which accounted for the depth I'd enjoyed for the last couple of hours. And there was a mechanical noise behind me.

I turned to look. I noticed a rusted iron grappling hook that had snagged onto my free wingtip. That's why it had sounded metallic. The wing was badly damaged on the aileron linkage where the hook had hung up, but at the moment I didn't care. A small diameter hawser tied to the hook ran across seventy feet or so of water to a little sixteen-foot motorized launch.

Two grubby old guys, I guessed fishermen, stared at me from the boat, with mouths agape. A cigar butt fell from the teeth of one. They looked stunned; they'd caught themselves a futuristic aquanaut—a pod man. One of them shouted something to the other one, something I didn't catch. I climbed completely out of the hatch and lay prone on the listing, slowly sinking pod, waving my hand at them feebly, beckoning them to me or I to them, and then they came to their senses and hauled vigorously on the line until my low-floating contraption was alongside their craft.

It took some effort to get me over the gunwale into their boat without sinking my glider. They were a bit rough dragging me across the rail, my knees and elbows bumping everything from thwarts to oarlock mounts, until they realized I had a hole in my calf, and then they took it a little easier. I wasn't bleeding as much as you might think, but it still hurt like hell whenever I bumped it, and would have to have some attention. And I expected to be bent, at least somewhat—pain in the joints or worse, from coming up too fast.

At my insistence the two guys stopped trying to cast off the pod like so much debris, instead lashing it loosely to the side in hopes it would stay on the surface...which it did, thankfully. And they started to head south toward the jetty in the main town, which was the logical thing to do since it would get me to a doctor the fastest. But I requested we gently tow the pod directly in to shore first, even though there was nothing there but a remote, narrow, rocky beach, and the detour would cost us a good half hour.

We grounded on a small gravel slope and I got them to drag and stash the pod as high as they could on some rocks and heavy driftwood logs that looked like they'd been there a long time, tying it there to reduce the chance of it disappearing on some high tide or in some gusty storm. I was pretty sure I wouldn't be able to come back for it right away, but I wanted a shot at reclaiming all the instrumentation and comm and pressure compensation systems inside it.

While we did this—that is, while they did this—one of the fishermen picked up a battered handheld radio of their own and announced to some woman on the other end that they'd found me and were bringing me in. He said it in a very matter-of-fact manner, and I knew then for the first time that they'd been out there looking for me specifically. They knew nothing about aqua-gliding—had never heard of it before, they said—but still they hadn't been surprised to snag a guy in a pod eighty feet below by dragging a kelp bed with a hook. They were looking for me right there, in that area of water. I was fading in and out by this time, more exhausted than I'd realized, and of course still in pain, and I didn't press the point.

They were from further north than the kelp bed, but they brought me to the jetty in the town to the south. It took about forty minutes. Someone was waiting for us, evidently called by the woman they'd talked to on the radio, and as we came alongside, the sheriff's car pulled up on the street by the shore bollards. I overheard one of the fishermen telling the deputy that they'd been flagged down and alerted to my predicament by some stranger on shore, and had gone straight out—they knew where the kelp was, obviously, since they were fishermen—and had been throwing the hook starting at the south end of the stretch for quite awhile before they caught hold of more than kelp. They didn't mention anything about any sharks, and I didn't bother to tell anyone about that until later, because I didn't want to get into arguments about whether locals think sharks hunt there or not—I knew that at least one did—and it didn't matter anymore anyhow. I assumed that someone walking on the bluffs above had seen me somehow, maybe when I'd almost surfaced on one of my last turns—it was hard to understand how I could have been spotted, but I wasn't complaining. They took me straight to the town doctor, who shot a local into my leg and then pulled a fat three-inch splinter of varnished oak out of it, and bandaged it tightly. I could even limp on it, although he went down to the little grocery store and bought me a cane. He was a nice guy. He knew that the leg was the least of what I'd been through, and I think he could tell I had a very tiny bit of an air bubble problem already, because my elbow hurt too. There was nothing immediate he could do about that though.

Eventually a rescue boat appeared from the meet tug, out at the jetty. I walked out slowly and they took me back to my team, and cold beer, which was in strict violation of the doctor's orders, although I didn't figure breaking that rule was going to kill me if the rest of the day hadn't. The fishermen were well versed in missing persons at sea scenarios, and knew the meet organizers would be beside themselves with concern, and had found out the emergency meet frequency and made the call.

...except that the Meet Head had apparently also received a call earlier on the same frequency. That was strange. It had been garbled, like it was transmitted with a lousy antenna or from a great distance. Of course I now understand, as I sit here months later drifting in darkness and silence...but it's too late.

Bob and Rick asked me why I'd been anywhere near that kelp. I didn't give them a good answer. Now everybody knows.

Like I said, I made a limping beeline to the bar on the tug, doing my very best to avoid the score board, where I didn't want to see the zero that would be next to my name. But Alan blurted out the day's results before I could stop him. I was amazed to hear that Lunfer had not crossed the finish; I'd expected the ass to be the day's winner, celebrating at the top of his boasting lungs, gloating, getting stinking drunk. But he'd zeroed. I wondered for an instant whether he was out there stuck like I'd been, and a momentary pang of guilt almost hit me at the thought of being so focused on myself I hadn't considered and reported that possibility.

But they said he'd beached out a couple of kilometers north of where I'd been stuck. You can't beach a pod without trying to; you can bob to the top, but running aground high and dry is another thing. He'd beached, and had never even returned to the tug. They said he was right then drinking in some local hole up there, alone, sopping wet and pissing off the proprietor of the place, as though he'd spent the day swimming in the cold water in his street clothes. When I heard it, I registered it as nothing more than a big question mark and yet another example of him letting down his team and his sport, and of having no respect for anyone around him—of being a low class, worthless oaf. The guilt I'd almost felt had been very brief, what with everything that had gone down over all the years, and the memory of the long painful list of funerals; I knew my hate could never go away. If there had ever once been anything else, it was gone, and the only thing left between Brian Lunfer and me was distance.

As a precaution, because of the mild symptoms of the bends that I was exhibiting, they dragged me off the bar stool before the first draught had been poured, put a hard diving helmet on my head, and made me do a decompression dive down to the bottom that very moment. It was only a hundred feet there, which might be less than standard protocol for bent divers, but me and the tug's dive master went down with hoses, stayed there breathing surface-supplied air for...I don't even know how long, maybe around an hour...and then came up slowly, stopping here and there for a few minutes, wherever he told me. Joint pain is bad enough, but air bubbles clogging up tiny blood vessels can cause tissue damage...aneurisms, like in the brain. So I put up with the ritual and the shivering. And I guess it helped the gas bubbles dissolve out, because the elbow felt better later, and nothing else ached. Then I toweled off, had a couple of frothy ales, and went to bed.

Over the next couple of months I made a reasonably quick recovery, and returned to my two kids and my consulting for awhile. Rumors came back in subsequent weeks that Lunfer had pretty much destroyed his pod in trying to ground the thing in rapid flight, all for want of an immediate bottle of whiskey as I saw it, and had then gutted and discarded it and was poking around trying to buy another used pod off anyone who had one big enough for him.

I had to salvage all the gear from my own, which I did over a few months' time after paying those same two fishermen to go get it and bring it to the town, where I transferred it to a rented truck to get it home. They were guys who almost never spoke; although they objected, I gave them a little extra since they'd saved my life. After that I faded out of the comp scene for awhile until this week's meet—the Chilean Worlds.

CHAPTER SEVEN

Not sure, but there still may be a few people who know me, or who know who I am because of the sport of Deep Flying, who still don't know that Brian Lunfer is my brother. If so, I'm to blame for their ignorance; I did my best to hide the fact for the longest time. Only a few of my closest friends knew in the beginning, and they knew never to bring it up. I still see some of them looking sideways at me when I express my hatred for the guy, but hate is hate, and they know all the reasons. They witnessed some of the worst of them. For sake of the record I'll explain as much of it as the battery power will allow, because I never told my kids anything about it and I guess they should know. The rest of you can think whatever you want.

Brian has a different last name, obviously; he never used Farragut, and I was glad of that. We'd adopted him. He was from bad seed—their family had lived in some ramshackle place that resembled a bunker, down by the Little Miami River east of Cincinnati. At some point his father had been convicted of armed robbery and second degree murder and was sent to prison. While in, I guess he continued to be a derelict, because he either never got out or he bounced out and back in again. Last I heard he's still inside, even now. He's living proof that he wasn't framed or a so-called victim of the system.

This all happened a long time ago, so most of it I know only by hearsay. I was told not to ask or speak of it in our home, and honestly I didn't know enough to know what to ask anyway. Brian's mother disappeared with a drifter a year after his father was sent up...only to turn up dead of an overdose somewhere in northern Missouri within five months. They found out she'd blown town after six-year-old Brian was found wandering around the school yard just before dark one autumn night. No one had come to take him home. The situation was heart-wrenching to my mom, who talked my father into taking him in. Nobody else had ponied up, and she was one for adopting strays regardless of pedigree. My bright, hard-working dad, himself from have-not roots, knew it was that same instinct in her to which he owed their marriage, and he accepted her causes, whatever they were, as his own. Brian took the bunk below mine and everyone said he became my brother. I didn't like him from the start.

Mom died not that long after. Maybe a year and a half. It was rough. They always talk about girls needing their mothers, and how much daughters are affected by the loss of the family matriarch. But I have to say things began to fall apart in our home in a serious way when Mom died. Not instantly, but more of a relentless disintegration. She was pregnant and full term, and we were all pumped up to get a new sibling, but when the time came the so-called medical experts accidentally gave her some crap they use to abort bad pregnancies instead of whatever they use to induce labor. Mis-labeled, they said, as though reasons were excuses...as though the how and why could possibly address the loss. That strong, healthy baby kicked her to pieces trying to get out, before it died. And she lost too much blood and went with it. My dad said at least they were together, and that we'd stick together in this world and hook up with them again in the next, but it was all a show of false bravery, because the life went out of him. I was only eleven.

Brian seemed to take it a little hard too, although I wondered, even back then, because at first he just went quiet. I thought it was an act, or maybe that he knew deep down who his champion had been and feared for his own prospects, rather than mourning the loss of someone the rest of us really loved. And he began to change—to take nothing seriously, to do reckless things. He got in trouble at school constantly, he seemed to have no respect for anything established, like church or school or family rules...or anything with rules, for that matter...and he would steal. His teachers reminded my dad that Brian had lost three parents in succession and needed us to pull together and pull him out of it, but we were floundering ourselves, and didn't have much extra in the way of understanding, or fortitude, or hope. My dad vowed to carry on what Mom had started, and he treated us both as his sons, but it didn't have much effect as I saw it.

We stumbled on, got older, the usual broken family scene...kids fighting with each other and lone parent working to pay the bills and trying to pretend it was somehow hanging together. In some ways the loss of Mom brought Brian and I a little closer—at least...well, we fought, which meant we must have cared...and we started doing young boy stuff with each other, like exploring the creeks and farm fields around our home, fishing, pitching baseballs to each other and chasing down the fly balls...stuff like that. We built forts out of scrubby little fallen trees, had snowball fights, made bows and arrows from branches and saplings that grew in the woods behind the house. We learned physics by trial and error, how far rubber bands made out of truck inner tubes could stretch in summer vs. in winter, which tree wood was strongest and in what season, and what materials could be bent and still maintain elastic tension. We learned why bike spokes have to be uniformly tight and what time of evening raccoons come out.

Brian was reckless, as I said. But back then, in a way, I kinda thought it was funny. At the same time I disliked him for it too...in retrospect out of jealousy as much as because he was breaking my dad's stuff and getting us both into trouble all the time. But I followed him and some of his hare-brained impulses sometimes, enjoying the risk, I have to admit. His attitude fed my own latent need to rebel, and I could always pretend that it was his fault.

When I was twelve or thirteen we began to venture further into the countryside around our home. We'd have a couple of hours after school if the weather wasn't lousy, since my dad usually had to work really late, and in summer we had nothing but time. Some people may wonder how two guys from a little landlocked southern Ohio farm can have such a bond with water, but none of them know about quarries. And neither did my dad.

We began to visit the nearest one in the summer when I was in eighth grade, to fish, while Dad was at work in town. For extra money my dad let people graze a couple of small ponies in our five-acre pasture, and no one ever came to visit them or really take care of them, so we were the only people those animals knew, and we pretty much thought of them as our own. We'd ride them back along the serpentine edge of the woods, where it flanked the pasture, and then through a gap in the rusted fence into the neighboring corn field. The land rose and fell at the whim of the subterranean limestone ridge, until the ridge broke the surface like a stoic, silent, eternal wave, forming a low and crumbling escarpment. That's where the first quarry had been dug about a century before.

They'd pulled a lot of rock out of that pit to crush it for roads and for other construction needs, and it was deep. Maybe it got too deep to make hauling the stone out of it feasible, or maybe demand died when surrounding city growth tapered off or building methods changed. I don't know, but it was at least three hundred feet from top to its deepest point, and maybe more. Like the others that ran in a long daisy chain southeast from there, it was full of runoff by the time we discovered it. Mostly, anyway. Someone had noticed the clear deep water long before we did, and had dumped sturgeon and smallmouth bass into it and the other deeper ones. Both species thrived in the cold, clear blackness. We heard there were pike in one too, but we never confirmed it by catching any.

Maybe my dad knew of the quarries' existence...probably did...but he didn't know we were going to them. Fishing them was difficult, what with the height we had to stand above the water's surface, along the cliff-like rim. The tangle of dead and waterlogged trees here and there, under which fish would lurk and on which fishing lines would snag, was also a major problem. But still, with the aid of big-barbed hooks and stout braided lines we'd sometimes bring home bass for dinner, and once a long sturgeon, and Dad appreciated them, although we lied to him about where we'd caught them. He didn't know fish species or what kind of water each would need, and he thought we were getting them out of someone's farm pond.

In my teens I'd already begun to explore flight, although it was more like how Tarzan flies, and I thought of it as swinging from a square-rigger's spar down to the deck. Swashbuckling Errol-Flynn pirate stuff. I was no different from a lot of kids, except that I at least had the good sense to swing into a big pile of leaves—I'd swoop, let go, and time it to have a soft landing. I guess that's why I didn't scare off right away. Then Brian tried it, starting from a much higher branch and overshooting the mound of leaves of course, and hitting hard. He got up laughing and kicked the leaf pile until he was out of breath. He didn't care to ask whether I might want to jump again. I got ticked off at him. Thereafter he never got into my attempts to break free of the ground. He'd watch me silently for as long as his attention span would allow, whether I was making a kite or an early glider or trying one out, but he never followed suit.

Back to the quarries: In the summer when I was fifteen, Brian talked me into swimming in one of them. It was really hot, with grey humid skies and air so still you could hear bugs creeping through tall grass. A hundred degrees, and ninety nine percent humidity, which translates to discomfort enough to drive one mad. The nearest normal place to swim was an hour away in a car for which we didn't have a key, and he said we should go fishing, although that wasn't really what he meant. He insisted the air at the quarry would be cooler, and that stupid idea started to get into my head too—I pictured that dark water somehow cooling the space above it, until I imagined that the difference in air temp would set up a breeze. I was so desperate for a breath of moving air that I chose to believe it, and we rode the ponies back there. It never occurred to me that I was the only one who had brought a fishing pole until he suddenly stripped naked and said, "You first, dude!"

"You're crazy," I told him, "it's a thirty foot fall to the water." But I was looking at it.

He jumped. He disappeared under the surface for a full ten seconds, and when I saw him again he was whooping and splashing, taunting me, and it looked so good I followed suit. It was great; the water was clear and cool, and since there was no stream in or out, there was very little mixing. So the surface was of normal summer temperature, but the deeper you dove, the colder it got. We swam for two hours, not realizing until we'd had enough that the only way up and out was across at the other end, where the cliff was climbable and where our clothes were not. We swam over and drew straws and I lost, but he came with me anyway, climbing up the crumbling rock and then slowly hacking our way through thistles and brambles all the way back to where we'd stashed our stuff. We were lashed to ribbons but laughing like idiots, me because of the adventure of it and I believe Brian because of the probability of scars.

We got to where we'd go back there to swim frequently, whenever it got hot enough to make it worthwhile. We became smarter about it of course, first walking the ponies to the far side, which took too long for our tastes, so later rigging a knotted rope so we could climb up at the preferred spot. Now and then we'd swim one of the other quarries, but they were further from home and not worth the extra effort.

Two summers later I went back there alone, and dove in. Brian was somewhere else—I didn't know then but eventually figured out where he was spending his time when he couldn't be found. Anyway it was easy to climb the rope alone—we each had to do it ourselves even when both of us were there—and I wasn't worried about it. I guess it was so hot I wasn't thinking straight.

I jumped the thirty feet with a huge splash— always loved that part—and then swam until I was tired. It should have been quiet, but the humidity was so great that the sky had begun to overdevelop with dense, dark clouds. A flash of heat lightning in the distance, and the sound of my pony stomping and calling to me from above, alerted me to the fact that it was time to get out.

I made one more surface dive, intent on being able to go home and brag to Brian that I'd touched the bottom with my hand. Of course I was nowhere near the middle, so it would have been as false a claim as a brag could be, but none of that made any difference because down below, where it was too dark to see, I encountered a rotting corpse entwined in rusted barbed wire.

I knew it was a body of some kind the moment I touched it, and I freaked out, turning and kicking madly as I angled up. I went right into a big ball of barbed wire and got caught in it. I must have been twelve feet down or more. When you get snagged like that, you don't think straight. You thrash and rip instead of carefully and wisely using the twenty seconds of consciousness you probably have to unweave whatever has its hooks in you. I didn't demonstrate such patience—I ripped free in maybe two seconds and clawed my way to the surface, screaming because of the death below me and because of the taste of my own hot red blood.

I'd slashed through my left bicep, and it was bleeding like crazy. Cursing, I paddled weakly over to the knotted rope, oblivious to the mounting wind in the skies above my head. A quick try convinced me I'd never get up that rope with my arm the way it was, nor would I make it across to the far side to attempt any cliff climbing over there. Nearly fainting from the pain, and naked and beginning to shiver, I clung to the lowest knot with my good arm and hollered until the echoes came back to taunt me. The pony answered my first yell and then took to prancing and pulling against its tether above.

I don't know exactly how long I was there—maybe an hour, maybe two. I got weaker as my body temperature dropped, until I even stopped berating myself for not attempting the swim the moment it had happened. I tucked the torn bicep against my chest as hard as I could, fearful of having nicked the brachial artery which I knew was in there somewhere. Luckily I'd come nowhere near it, and obviously I'd not have lasted that long if I had, but I wasn't thinking straight. It was incredibly painful, that much I recall. At some point rain began to pelt down around me, not a heavy downpour in terms of gallons, but more like rifle shots—large droplets racing each other at light speed, to pierce the water's surface and cause high plumes of liquid rebound. The rain made irrelevant any lingering thoughts I might have had of getting dry and warm by dragging myself out onto a log somewhere. In fact I may have been better off where I was, below the surface, at least protected from the wind that now curled with surprising strength into the hole of the quarry.

A heavy splash a dozen feet behind me barely registered. I had a momentary thought that a rock had dislodged from the cliff above, caused by movement of the rope to which I clung, or that the pony had decided to jump. You can see my mind wasn't working at peak performance. I probably assumed I was hallucinating, as I didn't bother to turn and look until a hand landed on my shoulder.

Brian was there, in his underwear and shoes, but nothing else. As I pieced together later, he'd come home and had waited around, then looked at the stagnant heat and the missing pony and had taken a guess as to where I was, noting in his slow, dense way that I was breaking my normal pattern and that the weather was beginning to vent some pent-up energy. At some point he'd decided to see what was up—I chalked it up to him wanting in on any adventures I might have found. Well, I thought, if so then he got what he wanted.

He'd arrived at the quarry, looked over the edge, seen me and the red water, and had jumped. He told me to hang onto the gash in my arm and let him do the swimming. And he did. He took hold of my chin and let me stream out behind him. I thought I was the stronger swimmer, but he did this with some serious speed and power. He got me to the other side and out of the water, then tied his soggy shoes on me and taunted and yelled at me until I managed to climb my naked self up the sloping wall to the rocky rim. With nothing else to hold onto, nothing a guy would grab on another guy, anyway, he took hold of my hair in one fist on a couple of the steeper sections and pulled, to help me get to the top. Then we made our way around the rim to where the ponies were tethered. I was shaking uncontrollably at this point—probably had been for an hour—and didn't have much left. I was near hypothermic, now that I look back on it, and it wouldn't have been long before all the shivering in the world wouldn't have kept my body temperature at a life-sustaining level. They call it exposure, but it's essentially a relentless progression from the temperature of a living body to that of a corpse.

We must have looked a sight to behold, he in his jockey shorts and me in nothing but shoes and red streaks of blood, angling slowly around the rim of the crater in the wind and rain. But there was no one to see. He pushed our pace hard, looking at my arm and my pale, weak shivering, but he didn't say much other than the occasional oath when he'd step on a sharp rock with his bare feet or tear through brambles ahead of me so that I'd not get the additional welts. He was bloody too, long before we got around.

By the time we got back to the ponies I was beyond exhaustion. My clothes, laying in a heap, were completely soggy, but he'd stashed his jeans and shirt under a log before jumping into the quarry, so they were a bit drier. And he'd put his shoes back on before the leap, knowing I'd need them down there. That was a bit of quick thinking, I realize now. He had something of a wild look in his eye, I remember—not exactly the carefree, stupid, reckless dude that was his true nature. He handed me the driest of the clothes and I managed to get them on. He ignored the fact that he wore only underwear, and we rode. We kept to the edge of the woods, me hugging my pony's thick neck for the warmth, and made it to the shed behind our house in about forty minutes, and then went inside. Dad wasn't home yet. Brian got me a blanket, and some broth so hot it burned my throat, and then ripped up an old T-shirt that we tied onto my arm, and he started to look a little more relieved. He stoked the living room fireplace and I sat as close as I dared, and soaked up some heat. As soon as Dad returned from work, Brian told him he'd nicked me with a garden hoe while playing Kung Fu.

Dad cuffed him for it and rushed me into town; the doctor put a bunch of stitches in my arm. It hurt like hell and took a couple of months to heal. The scar makes it look like I once lost the whole arm in an airplane prop accident or something.

Neither then nor in all the years since did Brian ever ask me how I'd gotten into that predicament. I thought often about it for awhile, realizing that the bloated thing with the gooey entrails I'd encountered in the depths had to be some hapless deer or livestock carcass, and eventually I too stopped thinking about it. I never shared that part with anyone, not until now—the fact that I'd freaked out and all. I believe I did resent that Lunfer had had to save me, because I wrote the whole thing off in my mind as him being a show-off and basically covering up for wherever he'd been that afternoon to begin with, and I told myself that my bad luck was his fault for starting the quarry swimming in the first place.

We never talked about it. Ever.

CHAPTER EIGHT

I didn't do any swimming, fishing or kite flying for some months, until long after my arm healed and I got some confidence back. Instead, in my spare time I began to study kite and airfoil design, and ship-building—how they used to do it, how they'd make the whaling boats, how the Norsemen had built theirs. I drew out and made model after model of airfoils and hydrofoils, and my dad would sometimes sit in the evenings and help me, or read the great seafaring tales while I worked on gluing up some model. We got closer over the time we spent imagining our similar fascinations. Dad was very much a romantic in his own right; he'd built vessels when he was younger and felt the pull of those years on his heart and mind. His favorite stuff when we were both absorbed in the evenings was Chapman's Piloting and Seamanship, for a contemporary title...and both the Odyssey and Iliad for old Greek myths of course, and Gordon Pym by Poe...some of Jack London's south sea stuff, Kirk's Fishermen...and Hemingway. Old Man and the Sea—goes without saying. And he'd read whatever he could get his hands on about Columbus' voyage, Cook's routes and trials, and even sometimes haul Moby Dick off the shelf, although I found Melville hard to wade through. Whatever he had in his hand, he'd pick sections completely out of order, more for their thrilling seafaring detail than their role in some larger human drama, and read them while I asked questions or speculated...or just pictured it.

Brian never took part in this interest, or so I thought. Often he was gone, and Dad would ask where he was, and I confess I wasn't very good to my brother in those moments. I'd quip something like, "probably stealing TV sets" or "maybe in jail." When he was home and my dad and I were talking about sailing, he was always out of sight—just barely, and still within earshot. He hovered, to the point of seeming like he was spying. He didn't get between us, and once or twice I wondered if, after all these years, he still felt like an outsider in our family. There was something about how he kept his distance from Dad. And I think Dad felt a kind of distrust growing—he couldn't help but notice the behavior, and he assumed Brian was hiding something, or that he was very slowly bowing out...which may have been pretty much what was happening.

One Saturday Dad took both of us to a lake over in eastern Indiana, where he knew you could rent little solo and two-man sailboats. His idea was to share one—go out with one of us at a time for ten or fifteen minutes, to show us the basics, and then let Brian and I take it out together. But he soon decided to rent a second one so we could all be out there at once. The things only had one small sail, a triangular bit of Dacron with a couple of grommets in the corners, and barely enough room for two slim people to sit—just a fiberglass tub with a point on the front, really, and a thin stick for a mast, and a couple of ropes through cheap pulleys for hauling the little aluminum tube boom this way or that. No furling or unfurling of majestic sails here...the guy just clipped one edge of it to D-rings welded to the mast, and it was ready to go.

Whoever was manning the tiller would sit aft...you know, in the back...and the other guy had to duck each time the boom swung across, to keep from being hit in the head. We fluttered around for awhile, in part because the breeze was so light, and also because we couldn't keep to a heading with respect to the wind. You always have to aim the bow of the boat relative to the air's movement, not to a point on the horizon or the opposite shore toward which you might want to go. If you enter a bit of air that's going at a different angle, or that's swirling, you have to adjust or it will play havoc with your heading, your forward progress, and even your stability.

Dad started with Brian and let me take one alone, because he knew I'd done some reading about how it's done. And it's true I picked up the basic idea pretty fast, picturing one particular diagram from one of the books in my mind. I couldn't tack or jibe yet of course, not on purpose anyway, but I could scoot along in one direction now and then, by setting the sail angle and holding the tiller still.

We managed to keep the boats more or less close to each other. Dad would call out suggestions and tips to me, while trying to put them into play himself. Brian seemed to be sitting or leaning the wrong way all the time, and Dad got a little frustrated. Once they tipped the boat over, until I paddled alongside—I wasn't adept enough to sail up to them under wind power—to help them right it. Another time Brian fell off; Dad had warned him that they were going to jibe and that the boom was about to swing across. It was a lightweight thing, just hollow aluminum rather than the massive wooden timbers used for booms on larger yachts, but a little whack on the head is still enough to startle a kid and send him backward over the side. I heard a splash and turned around to see Dad reaching back toward a colossal disturbance on the water behind him. I must have yanked the tiller as I turned, because my little skiff went crosswise to the breeze with me sitting high on the leeward gunwale, and I ended up in the drink too. If he'd been looking out the window, the guy who'd rented us the things must have been regretting the business right about then.

But Dad knew we were both wearing life jackets, and just shook his head and chased down my boat, and deftly brought them both alongside us. I realized for the first time then that he knew what he was doing. We climbed aboard and headed back to the dock, and then Dad climbed out and told us to get back out there and "figure it out." We dinked around for another hour, and that idiot Brian actually got his boat going a couple of times. It might have been the first time I realized he wasn't as stupid as I was sure everyone else thought—I began to see that half of it was an act, to get attention and to keep from being held responsible for anything. He kept following me, copying me in everything...right down to later, when he got into the Deep Flying sport.

Anyway on that day when we'd tried sailing for the first time, he did manage to get his boat moving, like I said, always watching me and trying to keep up, and all the while I was trying to tack, and jibe, and put some distance between myself and him.

Brian didn't fall in again, I don't think. He took to trying to ram my boat a bunch of times—his destructive nature as I saw it then, but maybe now I might say he was trying to stay in the mix, and was maybe a little resentful of my superior abilities and my relationship with my dad. He eventually lost interest and jumped overboard, swimming his boat back to the dock, frog-kicking with the bow rope in his teeth. At least he didn't leave the thing drifting in the middle for me or Dad or the rental guy to retrieve.

Judging by his demeanor on the way home and the fact that he broke our customary frugality by stopping to treat us to hamburgers, I think Dad was pleased with us that day. He clearly was more proud of me—as I always felt he should rightfully be—but he also seemed at least a little pleased that my brother had taken an interest in something, and had shown a little aptitude. After all, Dad had made a promise to Mom that he'd raise us both, that he'd give us both a chance in life. Dad cared about Brian, if only for Mom's sake I thought, and did his best to pull us all together with perpetual hard yard work, and a little evening baseball, wherein he'd hit us fly balls in the pony field and let us chase them down until darkness overtook us all. He could hit the ball. And now and then he'd cave in to our insistence that we go for a day hike in the steep broken terrain of Fort Ancient, which was an old Indian burial ground site and state park a little to the northeast, or for an early morning try for bass or carp at Rocky Fork Lake.

Brian did poorly in school. It started...well, before he came into our household. They said he'd begun with a bad attitude. He had immediately earned the label of 'slow learner,' and the kids mostly called him a 'retard,' mimicking him slurring his speech and lurching around with his peculiar dazed, uncomprehending look. But the teachers insisted that he started to show a marked improvement after Mom adopted him. What I saw in those years would have been hard to describe in constructive terms. I don't ever recall the guy doing his homework, which made it amazing that he didn't fail every test his pencil hit. Overall, his report card was never anything above disappointing, and when we both brought them home to get them signed, it used to tick me off how Dad would try to dwell on positives for Brian that just weren't there. There were always warnings and special sessions Dad had to deal with, speaking with teachers on disciplinary issues—Brian would get into fights, or be accused of stealing little things from other kids or damaging things like kids' clothing or books...one time it was a teacher's car in the school parking lot, another time the bus seats with a bent fork, yet another a classroom window...and as often as not the accusations fell just short of being provable, but the evidence was mounting up year by year, and Brian's reputation and behavior were disintegrating by the month.

One time he hit a kid in the eye, and then when the fight went to the ground, bit him— claimed the kid had said something about me. I forget the details, but when confronted by the Principal I told the truth about how he'd sucker-punched the guy. And he had. Brian got in big trouble and we were both held until Dad came to pick us up after school...and Dad did not smile at me or absolve me. His frown melted my air of impunity; I didn't understand why.

As elementary school gave way to ninth and tenth grades, Brian's reputation escalated downward. He was the lumbering, leering trouble-maker, the stupid one, the one you just know is a bully. No respect for rules, no intention to excel in any way. He distinguished himself only through failure and defiance. As I said, he did almost no homework...and yet he continued to be promoted, grade by grade, and his teachers evidently always had something encouraging to say to Dad that I never heard until much later.

Dad did his best to make a family of us. I have to say those days could have been worse than they were. He hid his own broken spirit and held us together as best he could. I've come to realize over the years that that's heroism—that's courage. This nonsense about saving the world with one daring deed is fiction; real courage is long, slow, and tenacious. Real heroism takes endurance.

I grew to love my dad without realizing that that's what it was. Boys don't dwell on such things, although we sure as hell feel them. And so the general embarrassment and dislike for Brian that I felt in those years descended into the first stage of hatred for what he did to Dad.

CHAPTER NINE

Brian got arrested, and it was Dad's ultimate undoing. I guess I must have known in my gut that Dad loved Brian too, or I'd never have seen that my embarrassing, reckless, stupid, delinquent brother was causing him so much pain. I didn't really want to know that Dad considered Brian his son, but I guess I knew.

Lunfer was around sixteen, or maybe not quite—I started to call him by his true last name about that time, probably hoping to disassociate myself and my dad from him in the minds of the kids at school and others we knew. I was in my senior year in high school. Brian cut school often, and I knew, but didn't care enough or want to care enough to tell my dad. But pretty much everyone at school knew too, and there were teachers who told Dad. He talked to Brian

I'm sure, out of earshot of me usually, but things didn't change.

At some point Brian had somehow gotten involved with a trashy older woman who lived in the Moss Creek trailer park. I have no idea how that started. Everyone knew the woman was married—she was well known around town, and even attended church daily, dressing in too tight, far too short skirts for her age and for church and for the town...almost like trolling for action while attending a house of worship. Her husband drove tractor-trailers, long-haul, to both coasts; he was away for days and weeks at a time, and was surely no monk himself, judging by how he carried himself the infrequent times he was seen around.

It became apparent when the rumor mill got going that teenage Brian, built like a high school football player although never having shown the character to try to make any teams, was dropping in on her several times a week. As I said, I knew he was cutting school, but I didn't much care, and I didn't know what he was doing or where he was hanging out. He'd been...finally...held back in the eighth grade, so at sixteen he was still a freshman and state law still required him to be in school.

Anyway one afternoon, like anyone far short of genius could predict, the husband came home to the seedy-looking trailer and caught my dear brother drinking beer naked on the sofa. The woman was in a robe or something, I think doing some drug or other in the back room. The guy went back out to his beat-up pickup, got a hunk of rusty steel rebar that had been riding around in the back of it for a couple of years, came back in, and tried to brain Lunfer with it. But Brian was younger and quicker; he dodged and grabbed a chair, and swung it at the guy, and the guy went down. He hit his head on the corner of something, broke his neck, and two days later he died.

The woman was out of it in the bedroom the whole time, according to Brian, but still testified that Brian had been the attacker. She was probably thinking insurance, or civil damages from us, or who knows what—certainly any theories that the blushing wife was protecting her reputation were preposterous. And they didn't find the rebar to corroborate Brian's story. If he was telling the truth then she must have tossed it in the scummy little pond down the slope behind her trailer, along with her stash of drugs. Brian was convicted of some kind of manslaughter, went into a juvenile detention facility, and didn't come out until four years later, except for an afternoon to contaminate the emotional atmosphere of Dad's funeral.

When I tell you I hated Brian for what I saw this thing do to Dad, I'm understating it. Dad's health went down like a stone in a well. He'd lost Mom, and then must have felt he'd failed his last promise to her, to raise us both to be men of character and strength. Brian was clearly headed for a penitentiary life and I couldn't stand him, which now that I think about it didn't help either. On the day we got a report from the juvenile prison that Lunfer had gotten into a knife fight with another under-age inmate, Dad had a stroke that night.

I didn't know what was happening. He was sitting with this weird, almost catatonic stare at the dinner table, first unresponsive and then muttering something nonsensical about a dented tin can on the table that wasn't even there. I asked him if he wanted to lie down and he didn't respond, so I helped him to the couch and put his feet up. I went into the kitchen, to the land line, and called the emergency number to get an ambulance on its way; when I returned to the sofa my dad was already in a full-on coma.

I tried to find a pulse and wasn't sure if I could or not. I didn't know what I was doing, but emulating movies and such, I pounded his sternum and checked for breathing with a small mirror in front of his nose and mouth, to see if it fogged. It seemed to, but then I was seeing through eyes wild with moisture and fear.

He never woke up. Strangely, no one ever had to administer a proper CPR, since his pulse and breathing were still there when the ambulance arrived. They got him on a respirator, but later said the damage the blood clot had done to his brain must have interrupted heart function and that I'd probably shocked things into restarting with whatever I'd done. They congratulated me...for what, I could never figure out, because I'd failed.

Dad stayed there, in that coma, for more than five weeks, which is the attention span of an insurance company. My dad...who had raised me and stood by me and loved me...guided me...dreamed with me.... He'd have never left the bedside, had I been the one lying broken there, and so neither did I. His body would sometimes turn his head or twitch an extremity, which I tried my damnedest to interpret as a good sign, but they all seemed to go far out of their way to see those things in the most negative possible light. Experience, they said. Brain stem; brain waves. Statistics. Hospice—just a pretty name for euthanasia. "Learn to move on," they advised. They all seemed to think they were giving me the gift of reality, of practicality; they were so smug in their presumed superiority of attitude. And they were never able to grasp the incredible value of hope, even if it doesn't pan out.

I realized then, and still know now, that for all their medical fact memorization, they were simply ignorant, and two-dimensional, and self righteous, and had grown incapable of seeing life and devotion in noble, romantic terms. I had no hate left for them; it was all held for Brian Lunfer. And I never realized I could, and would, come to hate him even more in my life, about a decade later.

CHAPTER TEN

I didn't sell the farm. Couldn't bring myself to eradicate the only place I could picture my childhood, my mom, and my dad. I leased the tillable land to a local farmer and the house stood empty while I went off to Miami University; I rented a room near campus during the week but would go back to the farm from time to time, to work on a glider or have a simple dinner at the family table alone.

Before Dad died, I'd already done some significant hang gliding, as I mentioned before. I'd thought he knew little about what I was doing, and that's true enough, because I tried not to mention to him the strong air stuff or the longer cross country flights I'd done while he was at work. He did know something, though, because he'd caution me to be careful sometimes, out of the blue. And word must have gotten around—like when I landed in a field way down by Pisgah, which turned out to belong to a farmer we knew. Dad asked me once to set up my "kite" on the back hill, and then marveled at what I'd created. Of course he'd assumed it was my design, and I had to come clean and admit I'd copied existing planforms for the most part, and had bought some kit pieces that I couldn't make myself. But still, that didn't deter his respect. I hooked in and launched so he could see how it was done, gliding a couple of times gently down to the bailout clearing at the little thirty foot hill's base, and he was amazed. He actually had some good suggestions about launch technique, right off the top of his head, which I used thereafter for a little additional safety margin. And like me, he saw the glider as an approximation of sailing on the high seas. We all go with what we dream and what we know, and I guess the fascination for the seafaring life was in both our DNA.

Another time when I was out there doing some repairs on the thing, he came home early and walked out to have a second look. We were inspecting the simple prism-shaped airframe and running our hands across the glider's sleek leading edge cloth. Dad shook his head and smiled, and said, "my amazing boys." What blew me away was the plural in that remark. What had my stupid, reckless, non-brother ever done?

But I was to learn much later that Dad had known something I didn't, and, all promises to Mom aside, the reasons why he'd hung in there with Lunfer and had put up with all the guy's crap.

After Dad died I'd sometimes go stand on the little hill from which I'd launched the first time he'd seen my glider. I'd pretend that we were chatting about flying and sailing. I'd field his questions and ask him some of mine, and imagine little give-and-take visits there. It helped. I missed him.

Lunfer never came back there, or not that I ever saw. He had the nerve to leave me a phone message at one point, babbling about not having been told Dad was in a coma until it had been too late, and that he wished he'd had a chance to visit him in the hospital—something about wanting to try to "wake him up." It's true I'd never told him, in those five weeks; he was the reason Dad had been there in the first place. I guess they pretty much just inform inmates when a family member dies, not when they're about to. Anyway, I never responded to the message he left.

As I said, I went to college in the autumn of the year Dad died. Lunfer spent another two years in the juvenile facility and was then released. He got a job and entered a trade school—welding—and seemed to settle down a bit, although he didn't marry. He wasn't exactly the responsible type. For awhile I didn't know who he hung out with or what he was into, or where exactly he lived.

It was in the spring of my freshman year at Miami U that I discovered the aqua-gliding concept and began to put that new obsession into play. Dad would have loved the idea, had he been alive. I imagined he was watching, fascinated and pleased; that thought partly fuelled my passion for it, to be honest. Maybe the void left by his passing helped make the sport happen, I don't know. Maybe it was more overt than that—maybe it was Dad who fed me the inspiration from the Great Beyond. I do know that someone had to have been protecting me, because I began a life of very dicey moments and always came out of them with nothing but a scar here or there. I've deep-flown thousands of miles and gone deeper than you can imagine—deeper than I've admitted to anyone...and then what happened today, which makes everything else pale in comparison.

Well, college was an interesting time for me—I got a mechanical engineering degree, graduating in the top maybe seven percent or so, and could have done better than that if I'd been focused entirely on grades. But that was okay because at the same time I was forging a place for myself in the world with the aqua-gliding thing. I had my share of notoriety in school, made some good friends...and there were girls...I have to say I liked the attitudes of the sophomores in general, because they weren't afraid to admit they'd heard of me, but still they had some personality going on themselves. They were a nice blend, in that sense. I dated Patricia Trask for awhile, until she changed majors and left the school for somewhere out west, and then Sara what's-her-name...Parthaus...until Alan saw her at a Greek party making out with some loud, obnoxious guy from the wrestling team, and I stopped calling.

As I said, in my senior year I met Adrienne. It was early May—I was just about to graduate, and, truth be told, that timing pretty much clinched my decision to go ahead and do some grad school work, so that I could spend more time with her. I missed that first summer competition season, but spent the time well, designing a better pod and studying strategies. I did what nobody else was doing yet, absorbing scuba diving lore and all, because I wanted to extend my aqua-gliding into deeper water, to give me more options. And it did pay off—the year after that, I wiped up the rest of the world, scoring almost half again as many points as the nearest rival. It was kinda like the guy from Finland...Siitonen?...who first began to apply skating technique to cross country ski racing—he did it mid-race...used it to come from behind and blow them all away...and then Koch and eventually the rest of the field began to do the same thing in subsequent years. And that's sorta what happened to me. I had a huge Deep Flying advantage that next year, what with my beefed up pod and ability to go to greater depths, to fly alone, to glide farther and such...and because I'd spent a year absorbing all that lore from the scuba crowd. I'd invented the concept, I knew pods, I knew flying, and now I knew depth...I was in a league of my own. Of course little by little the others started to figure out what I was doing, and catch up. I always had to pull something new out of my hat. That's how I kept winning the championships, although the margins became more and more narrow, as my pioneering strategies got less and less revolutionary. The sport was maturing. I was compelled to do more and more dangerous, unthinkable things. Like this race, today.

Got ahead of myself there...battery is still holding on...maybe starting to sag a little, but I can't think of any better way to drain it and be done with it than to get this whole story out...I want to talk about Adrienne a bit more. She's so much of this tale. Karina and Jeannie, if you ever come to listen to this, it's the story of how your Mom and I decided to...to form our family. We had that first glorious summer together. That's when Adrienne realized how much in love I was with the romance of sailing. I've wished a thousand times in recent years that she'd never seen that fascination in me, that I'd talked about movies or blueberry pie or the Cincinnati Reds shortstop or who cares what, in that first year. But I didn't; I planted in her head what I was all about...I invited that dark cloud into our home, before our home even existed. I was egotistical, always talking about myself and what I loved.

And avoiding mention of what I didn't love.

We spent a lot of time outside in those months, after her broken leg began to mend, anyway. I think she'd been a little bit into bicycling before her accident, and the open road began to beckon once she could walk easily. Her doctors were all for it, since it was basically rebuild therapy without high impact...as long as she didn't take a fall of course. Naturally I went along with it. Her parents trusted me for reasons I'll never understand, and I think they appreciated the diversion I provided while she got her full strength back. We'd do afternoon rolls through county parks and whatnot, usually with a pack full of lunch and picnic blankets strapped to my back, and occasionally with a fishing pole as well, since most of those parks had little lakes. We'd kill the warmer hours tossing stones or acorns into the drink, or sometimes taking pictures through a long lens she liked to carry, if the clouds or sunlight were unique in some way...you know, generally just spending time together. I liked it; it was a welcome change of pace from the hectic competition circuit. I almost felt lazy; hedonism had never been part of my ways.

As far as the fishing went, we never caught very much, but then it goes without saying that we weren't all that focused on fish. I remember we did somehow manage to pull in a channel catfish about fifteen inches long once—can't remember what we used for bait, but I do recall it was in broad daylight...mid-afternoon...so I always thought of it as a catfish that liked to break the rules. Kind of a Brian Lunfer of catfish, maybe. Anyway we were going to let it go...I remember asking Adrienne to hold it out so I could get a photo first. Those things are slimy and ugly as sin of course, and she elected to operate the camera while I did the dirty work, so I held it far forward of my body, right into the lens, so it would look bigger in the picture. It ended up blurry, it was so close, which only added to the effect. I still have that photo somewhere I think.

On some of those little jaunts I'd occasionally find myself harking back to my younger years, recalling fishing the old quarries with Brian. He and I had been very intent on catching game fish, but had also chased pretty much anything big, including catfish and carp, when the opportunity had presented. Lazy picnic fishing was fun, but every now and then I found myself missing the real thing, too.

Adrienne and I would often end our days that first summer on the porch swing at her house. Summer heat would fade to low light, then to a welcome coolness when the humidity just started to precipitate out as dew...and finally to a gentle nighttime chill, with loons crying from the woods, which was the part I loved most. I'd put my arms around her and we'd watch the lightning bugs twinkle. Sometimes we'd sit instead in the back yard, on a long folding chair, where we could face a big grassy field in which the blinking yellow points of magical light now and then made a cloud so dense you'd swear the Rapture had come to envelope us all. And maybe it had.

But nothing lasts forever.

I remember once making the mistake of commenting to her how Brian and I had used to go fishing. Her reaction was to take unusually keen interest, and to strongly encourage me to call the guy up. Her "encouragement" could easily have been spelled n-a-g-g-i-n-g, from my perspective; it was clear she sensed that he and I were estranged, which didn't take a genius to recognize, given that I never talked much about him and always found some way to change the subject. She knew he embarrassed me. I don't know if she realized that I blamed him for elbowing in on my childhood, and for my dad's death. And neither of us could have known that that was small potatoes compared to what Destiny had in store.

As I'd said earlier, we got officially engaged eventually...around May of the following year, and a couple of months after she'd said no to my early spring proposal. She told her parents our plans right around the time I transitioned from grad student to a full-time job at a contract engineering company, to do solid modeling computer work. That kind of work is fun, and I was finally going to have a decent income, so once I was pretty sure it was going to happen, I caved in—quite willingly, mind you—to the previous winter's hints from her family that we begin to think about our futures. That's the way I told it afterward, anyway, to my bachelor buddies; a guy has to pretend to save face, after all.

We were married in October, after only about a five-month engagement...a relatively big wedding, given the short notice, and I have to hand it to her parents for pulling it off and giving us that. It included a church ceremony, with the traditional feel, and a huge outdoor party that lasted through dozens of speeches, hours of music, and until the hundreds of colored paper lanterns burned their thick slow candles down to the nubs. I was forced by her mom to invite Brian, and was amazed that he showed up. He wasn't dressed up much, but he didn't drag any cheap floozies through the event or try to hit on the catering girls, either. I accepted his bracing punch in the arm from my position in the receiving line, never once forgetting that I wished Dad could have been there in his place.

Fourteen months later Adrienne announced that she was carrying our first, who we named Jeanne about a day before she was born. Maybe it was procrastination, or maybe we just imagined too many options, but it really did take us that long to decide. Adrienne took long walks over those months, to the great health benefit of mother and daughter alike.

Jeannie was the glow that made the world a paradise. I laugh to think back how parental we were...we took videos of her doing anything and everything—stretching her arms, yawning, reaching out to touch little stuffed doggies and froggies and duckies, burping, smiling, snoring. Imagine, if you will, the dynamism delivered by a video of a baby snoring. I don't know if we ever watched any of them at all, because weeks became months and years, and the new material that needed to be filmed was non-stop. I can't imagine how many terabytes of stuff we accumulated...probably have gigs and gigs of yawning footage alone, all absolutely identical and yet all of it seemingly "must-capture" material at the time...but it doesn't matter. The point was that we were happy. Adrienne was not only my love, she was my friend, and even kinda like the sister I never had...and now I had a tiny little sister too, lying there in the crib with her thumb in her mouth and one chubby little finger hooked over her nose. Together these two filled an empty hole in my soul; I thought of them as the only family I was ever meant to hang onto.

Nineteen months later, we added Karina to the team, and the alternating quibbling and hugging between the two little ones never failed to crack me up. I was quite possibly the worst father ever—I couldn't be stern or firm to save my life. Those two—correction, those three—could get away with anything under the sun. They took advantage of me every possible way, but then that's what Dads are for. I smiled especially when the little ones would fall asleep leaning against me on the sofa, or in a little tent when we began to do family camping...I'd be pinned down for fear of awakening them. That's love, right there, I'd remind myself, as my leg or arm would go numb.

In time Adrienne's job with the Chicago publisher blossomed into some wonderful things. She actually got sent to Washington once to cover a press release given by the President, and another a year later by the Secretary of State. The second time the kids and I went too. It seemed to me her work nicely balanced factual elements with uncertainties. I liked that—of course I was biased. But she really was unique in that even the most partisan readers seemed to feel informed and a little mellowed by her reports. And when she secretly finished a novelette and presented it to me as a gift one year, it blew me away. I hadn't even known she was writing anything! I kidded her that it was more "foofie" than something I'd have written, but I was proud...people really liked it. Everyone but her, actually. She decided she wasn't satisfied with it, and said her plan was to re-do it as a screenplay. I don't think that project ever quite got finished though.

I left my job with the contract engineering outfit and devoted full time to aqua-gliding, stepping up my consulting efforts, spreading my talents around the top three pod manufacturers, until Sonnenwende, who was a high end boutique pod maker at that time, realized they could probably dominate if they could ramp volume and lead technologically. I knew pods, and more importantly I had a formal background in mechanical engineering, which meant I could work with their vendors on improving manufacturability. Yield. They had their eye on cranking out a revolutionary new pod design that would blow away all others and be more affordable to boot. I have to say I fanned that flame, because I wanted them to court the hell out of me. I wasn't sure a single design could dominate as thoroughly as all that, but even if we were thirty percent successful it would be a huge boost to them, and the trickle-down into a parallel recreational product line would bring a ton of new participants into the sport. All that extra interest would spawn new mini-meets everywhere, televised trials, sponsorships from mainstream product companies...cereal boxes, trading cards...hell, I thought, we might even become an Olympic Exhibition Sport some day.

There were still a ton of hydrodynamic opportunities the sport hadn't incorporated yet, so pod performance advancements weren't going to be difficult to drum up. Custom designs made by hand that could beat the mass-produced thing Sonnenwende had in mind were always going to be possible, of course, but they had their heart in the right place, and I liked that. They came out of a culture of innovation and excellence in other water recreation product spaces, so I was convinced they'd stay the course for this new thrust. They wanted something that competitors could not afford to pass up if they wanted a snowball's chance at winning—the general perception of that, anyway. Hang glider designs had gone through similar cycles at times, so the vision made sense. And they wanted to name the thing after me.

I pushed back on that last bit, citing humility grounds, but secretly I knew that not all of my design ideas were proven enough to roll out with the company's money, and in all honesty I still had ideas of one day rolling out a design of my own. But I had to blow away a major world title first; up to then the sport had been small enough that my titles were still considered niche sport wins. I wanted to see the major growth, the explosion, the world media infatuation, and then dominate in front of a crowd of billions glued to their tubes.

But I negotiated an exclusive consulting role at Sonnenwende, and it paid really well. Tied to it were requirements that I place in the top three in several meets a year and that I amass a minimum number of circuit points, so competing was essentially the highly visible part of my job. I went to Class A meets, four to six of them per year on average, to maximize the points available to me, trusting that I could still dominate in those higher-skill crowds even though I wasn't doing two races a month. That strategy was meant to give me more bang for my travel buck and more time with Adrienne and the kids.

I knew Alan in college, but it was at the Caribbean Classic that I met Marc and Paul. I think I met Rick later, in the Lake Huron trials, and Ted later still...met Bob and Will at an awards dinner in Livorno, where they cracked up a hundred Italian and Euro pilots with a skit about being shipwrecked in a pod with Swedish girls, who it seems are obligatory characters such fictional scenarios must always include. The Italians in particular, ever appreciative of tales of amore involving northerly blonde folk, were in stitches, because the story line didn't quite go as expected. I was on the floor too; it was so funny, so well done.

Anyway I noticed that Alan, Paul and Marc flew well in the Caribbean. They were pretty good, lacking only in time spent in the sport. They definitely had the aptitude, and more or less without the gonzo macho "go for it" formulaic focus that passes for skill so often these days. Guys go out and take unbelievable chances, running compressed air reserves down past zero on the gauge, or running too deep for too long and then surfacing too fast, trusting those cheesy thirty-dollar air mixture compensators to keep them from getting the bends...cutting across areas with way too much vertical reef in hopes of shaving off a few minutes...stuff like that. Nothing as bad as Brian in the Outer Banks, but still they fly without much margin, relying on the ninety-nine percent chance it'll work out, and when they score well they strut around like they're really good, really knowledgeable, really skilled, when what they are is really stupid. In hang gliding they get the same kind of guys—they surface every couple of years and run up a string of good scores and set the circuit on fire...golden boys, up-and-comings, new kids in town...and then one day when they've cut across long stretches of unlandable terrain a couple dozen or more times, that ninety-nine percent statistic lets them down and they fly themselves into a two-hundred-foot

Ponderosa Pine and die, or end up as a vegetable. In Aqua-gliding they impact reefs or get the bends or something, and usually they're recovered without their expensive pod. They end up playing golf or bowling the rest of their lives, or betting on football from their sofas.

Marc and Paul and Alan...especially Paul...were different. They were more like me...in fact Paul took it to an art form. They intended to excel by force of knowledge and sound decisions. They weren't placing in the top ten, but then they didn't have the best gear, either. It was going to click for these guys at some point, and even I was learning things from them, like the value of patience when opportunities are just hanging back all day, never presenting themselves. Paul had an enormous capacity for patience, for concentration, and more than once I saved my own flight by repeatedly chanting to myself that I was him.

I talked it over with these guys first, then went back to Sonnenwende and made a strong case for sponsoring an entire cadre of factory pilots. Hit the sport with an army, I said, give the very strong impression of momentum. Make sure to use guys with the right attitude, and I had the very ones. Sales would follow, I promised, and I bet my nonexistent reputation as a salesman on it. We had to put in an appearance at almost every meet, no matter how small, even before our new pod design was rolled out.

My sponsor argued over the cost of doing that, but I suggested a deal based mostly on commission, for those guys. They'd been thinking that the reps could be our presence out there, but the problem is that reps don't always fly, or fly well. Newer entrants into the sport get jazzed over flying with an actual "professional" pilot, a competitor sent by a manufacturer and backed by them. Anyway, Sonnenwende took the bait and we signed those three guys on my recommendation. They each got access to the factory store room of spare aqua-gliders, and we began to custom-outfit one for each of them, based on height, weight, flying style and such.

Will, Rick, Ted and Bob came to the team later. Rick and Bob had come out of other sport racing backgrounds and were ready to step it up. Ted found us on his own, but fit right in. Will had been flying Cork Class, which was absolute blatant sandbagging for a guy of his promise. It wasn't that he was focused on trophies or anything like that; he was simply not all that tuned in to the comp part of things. It was the social aspect of the aqua-gliding world that had attracted him, and he was just flying, laughing it up, hanging out at the après-race party keg spigots, winking at every girl that walked by, and living the life. In the interest of being true to his potential, I pulled him into the serious fold and ended all that...for which he never forgave me.

So we slowly put together the whole Sonnenwende team. We'd fan out to greater and lesser meets, but of course always meet up at the biggest and best. These guys became my new brothers. I was flying Unlimited class, whereas they were mostly working Formula Four heats, for the time being anyway, but otherwise we flew the same water when we could, and tried to keep our personal ambitions from interfering with our willingness to help each other along.

I have to say I still kept some of my more inspired theories and secrets to myself, like the turbulator screw heads on my hand-made pod...and the strategy I used today. It was my livelihood and my right, I told myself—my family's future. Truth is, it was also my ego driving those decisions, and my strong need to annihilate one competitor in particular.

CHAPTER ELEVEN

For a long while, my teammates, almost to a man, were as clueless as the rest of the sport that Lunfer was my brother. Adrienne never mentioned it. We'd all have barbecues and dinners and such...get together to watch World Series games on TV...as I said, my team became my family. But I still kept that from them.

Brian Lunfer is not quite the idiot everyone always thought. He had me going for many years, and I was the closest one to him, but at some point I realized he wasn't entirely dim. He has lurched and lumbered around all of his crass, wasted life...taking nothing seriously, breaking rules, most likely stealing or dealing, getting in fights...and always with that irreverent leer on his face. He adopted the gait, posture, and drawl of a lazy, rebellious bully way back in our school days. He was a cliché—the poster boy of stupid physicality, of learning deficiency, of delinquency. In high school the kids named the detention room the 'Lunfer Lounge.' Like fat guys are presumed to be socially wired and comical, like girls with acne and glasses have adjectives like "introverted" and "withdrawn" automatically added to them despite who they may really be, Brian Lunfer was deemed stupid on the basis of his mannerisms. He was the one everyone knew was most likely to end up in a juvenile detention center, which came true, and who was ultimately headed for max security state prison, which never quite. Not for want of him tempting it.

But he wasn't actually stupid. And as strange as it sounds, that fact earned him my eternal hatred.

He had very poor judgment, no one can deny...and a knack for getting into situations that had no graceful way out. It's possible that the persona he projected encouraged the world to discount his value and to throw the book at him, but then it was a persona he chose and cultivated, so as I saw it, it was still his fault. I don't know, maybe he acted the part because he believed it himself—maybe he too thought he was worthless.

Other than eighth grade, which they did more as a statement about accountability because he had done exactly none of the remedial summer work they'd prescribed for him, they never held him back in school. He managed to pass. Every year but that one. I'd heard someone say his math scores in the big state tests were off the charts. I'd always assumed that that was some kind of colossal joke—a chart has more than one "off" direction, after all—and it embarrassed me when the other kids would taunt me that way. I'd secretly blame him for drawing all that mockery and disrespect to our family. Now I look back, and I remember my dad having so many meetings with Brian's teachers, always followed by renewed efforts to check and guide his homework...efforts that perpetually failed because Brian never did any. But they saw something in him, although I didn't know. Dad felt a responsibility to raise the guy, to let Mom's pet project run its course. He was honoring her. But Dad also took some kind of strange pride in Brian. I think, looking back, that that must have sunk into my head somehow, and must not have sat so well with me. Mom and Dad were mine, you see.

I begin to grasp all that a little more clearly now. This morning I didn't. I still hated. I've always hated. All the things he did that ruined my life, all the unbelievably bad judgment, the irresponsible behavior...there's more, as you'll see, much more...I think I might have been able to forgive stupidity, but never fake stupidity...never intelligence.

Lunfer spent a couple of years after high school just kicking around, holding odd jobs, like pizza delivery and stuff, just enough to buy gas for a loud, cheap, beat-up car that looked like it had been "frankensteined" out of stolen parts...and he lived off of some divorced woman in Hamilton for half a year or so...and then for some reason got an apartment by himself and did one year of junior college. I don't know—never cared—what prompted that. Don't even know what he studied. It couldn't have been anything he was very good at, because he washed out soon enough—possibly nobody was advising him, and possibly he was too lazy to think his future through himself. Anyway he then worked as a mechanic I think, and I heard got into another trade school for a short time, all of which landed him in a machine shop. Somebody once told me that place did precise high-end custom work on light alloys; when I thought about it at all, which was rare, I always assumed Lunfer had to be the guy who emptied the scrap bins and dragged the raw metal chunks into and out of the warehouse so that skilled craftsmen could do their thing. But I never knew, or asked.

He must have done some truck driving in there somewhere, too; I probably have half of this out of order, but I'd hear little comments now and then from people I'd run into that he was on a long haul trip to one coast or the other.

It was in those years that he got nailed for drugs.

They say a lot of drivers do a lot of pills to stay awake, driving through the night, maybe to make up on the road time they'd spent with some floozy along the way...or to get to their destination sooner and score themselves some early delivery bonus money. Then half the time they blow the bonus on slot machines in Elko Nevada or somewhere, pumping in a hundred silver dollars in a matter of minutes. Stupid. Even guys with a supposed aptitude for math can get caught up in that lazy thinking, chasing the quick score and never getting anything for it but a chemical addiction. I don't know that Lunfer ever did any gambling, but the drugs part was right up his alley, reputation-wise anyway. So I wasn't all that surprised when two detectives came to interview me one Saturday morning, interrupting a nice little family breakfast I was having with Adrienne and the kids, asking a million questions about when I'd last seen my brother, how he lived, what his habits had been in our younger years, and where

I got my own money from. I had to trot out pay stubs and talk about what our rent was and what my car payments were and such. They pulled my consulting clients into the discussion to verify my income records, which in turn spawned some questions and some sideways glances at Sonnenwende, who wasn't keen on shouldering any scandals. I had to give my boss the whole repetitive litany about how I didn't know what it was about, that it may have to do with other people in the sport, that authorities could be fishing for small-time tax form inaccuracies...anything to disassociate myself in a personal way from the questions. Luckily the authorities never mentioned any names or reasons—they tend to keep their cards close to the chest—and I got by with my clients on plausible deniability. But secretly I knew Lunfer was still putting my reputation, and now my livelihood, in jeopardy. The guy was just a continual fly swimming in the soup.

And what annoyed me as much as anything, and probably more, was that Will came back to the factory one time after a low-points fun-fly meet in Sandusky to tell us he'd been edged out of a first place finish by a guy in a cork class recreational glider. Sonnenwende didn't love the sound of that, I have to say, especially since they'd outfitted us all with really good stuff and had their name emblazoned all over our hulls. Every one of us on the Sonnenwende team was recognizable by then. We'd fan our best guys out to most of the big meets, when they occurred, and try to send up-and-coming comp pilots like Will to the less serious events—a lot of pilots new to the sport began their competition flying at those, so of course it was in our best interest to impress them, and Will was good at making friends. It all worked well as a formula for presence, sales, and support of the sport.

So when Will came clean and admitted he'd been beaten by twelve seconds over a two kilometer course by a cork, our team reactions were...in this order...pump him for specifics, friendly ridicule, denial, more friendly ridicule, and eventual dismissal of the news as a freak thing unworthy of further pondering.

And then our Sonnenwende sponsor very seriously asked who the pilot was who'd beaten Will. I started to smirk, assuming there was a joke in there somewhere about Will losing his spot on the team, when he opened his mouth and said, "Some unknown named Lunfer who flew his ass off."

Of course it was bound to happen in a story like I'm telling you, but when such a tale is your life, you don't see it coming. Brian had followed me into Deep Flying, and evidently had been attending little meets out there, in stealth mode, learning and improving without making it onto any charts. He'd gotten hold of some used piece of recreational junk on eBay or at a flea market, and had figured things out. Well, if he wanted to remain off the radar, that wasn't in the cards anymore; he'd won a meet against a sponsored, seeded pilot.

I was as angry as I was floored. This was my niche; why couldn't the guy carve out some other world for himself—some world that wasn't likely to include me? Like Federal prison. But he had to elbow in on my turf. It was going to make it hard to disassociate myself with him...in fact the guys all thought I had no living relatives, so I'd have to back-pedal as soon as the truth got out. And it would.

I contemplated waiting it all out—just letting the unknown new guy collect his one freak trophy and disappear into forgotten lore, but he did it again at Kentucky Lakes later that same summer. Again with the worthless pod, but he pulled some magic out of his ass and blew them away. They even re-measured his buoyancy, thinking he had some illegal advantage, but his pod came up clean. Not flight-worthy, since it had a wicked turn due to some bent linkage, but clean. He guffawed and told them he did have trouble with it going left all the time, but just avoided going right. Again, stupid...while somehow being brilliant. The guy became an instant household word within the sport, and I couldn't stand it.

They said he'd often countermand his own flight computer's calculations and just do complex final glide math in his head...even several turn points and many thermals out. They all started to mimic his lumbering gait, the brain-dead expression, the drawl, the drool, but they seemed to be doing it in the spirit of him being a celebrity, not the ridicule I knew he deserved.

The guy took second place the very next weekend in Boca Grande, and then won a third meet that year—still a lesser one, but all the same, by this time he enjoyed the stature of a rough-hewn cannonball on the rise. The national magazine couldn't get enough of photographing him; they ran a quote in which he supposedly said, "One way or another pilots got to get the job done." What a crock, I thought, what a vapid rip-off of a line from some Sergeant Nick Fury comic somewhere...if that sound bite passed for either wisdom or drama, then the world was a sorry place.

After his second-place Boca Grande showing, Sonnenwende had pulled us together for a meeting to say that until we had a better plan they wanted to stop sending pilots to meets in which he was entered, to avoid the embarrassment of being equaled or beaten by equipment that bad. They did ask me to go to one or two of those meets, knowing I'd still dominate, but I found good reasons to deflect and avoid. But in Lunfer's third full win, at the après-flight party the Meet Head apparently asked him basically what rock he'd crawled out from under—where he'd trained, where he'd been, what had compelled him to take up the sport to begin with. And, bless his heart, he publicly accredited his dear brother as the source of his inspiration.

This news hit the sport like a cobalt bomb. The phones at home and our office wing at Sonnenwende had to be disconnected for two days. The aqua-gliding rags of the world ran his drunken face on all their covers and website home pages...opposite my own. All kinds of presumptions popped up—everything from a pre-planned family dynasty that sounded an awful lot like a conspiracy, complete with officials pay-offs and leaking course maps to the guy in advance...to Lunfer being a poser, a media-chaser, and a liar. Hoping that last one would reign and let the scandal die out, I managed to dodge questions for about a week, and then Theresa Faulkland of the Enquirer cornered Adrienne and me in a quiet Vietnamese coffee shop one Saturday after stalking me for four days, and promised to tell it right if I gave her the scoop. I saw where it was all leading, and 'fessed up. Yes, he was indeed my...ADOPTED...brother. No, I'd had nothing to do with his flight training. Yes, I was as floored as everyone else. And...yes, damn it...I had great respect for the guy and looked forward to flying with him as this great sport continued to grow. That last part she wrote up pretty gracefully, considering I'd choked up a lung on it when it had come out of my mouth.

Naturally my client demanded an explanation for why I'd misled them, and of course I didn't have one that would really fly. There was some strain there—they were implicated in the public deception and didn't appreciate the embarrassment. I told Adrienne...Lunfer had a million other things he could have gotten into, a million other worlds he could have contaminated with his participation. But he had to keep gluing himself to me. Hadn't I made it clear enough when Dad had died that he and I were no longer connected? Of course she didn't understand.

So that's how my past had caught up to me. If I thought I'd left it all in the murky ethers of history, I was mistaken. There's no avoiding the smudges of our lives; we just have to face them head-on, own them, rise above them, defeat them. I made up my mind that if I couldn't keep him out of the world I'd carved out, I'd just run him out by so thoroughly eclipsing him that he'd fade away, one more also-ran in a sea of them. Let the guy be what Billy Carter was to his U.S. President brother—an insignificant tag-along...a mug shot on a cheap can of beer. I'd be my dad's noteworthy son. Me. Yes, that's how it would go.

Except it didn't. The lumbering, leering, vacant-eyed "retard," to coin the abusive grade-school word, was reckless enough to try anything, lucky enough to get away with it, and didn't seem to need a flight computer. Reports were that he left the thing, dead battery and broken display and all, on a bar stool on the tug as often as not. Yes, he'd won three meets that summer, but that doesn't tell the whole tale because he finished in the top five in several more. It was almost like the Boston Marathon in 1980 when Ruiz crossed the line first...except that you can't cheat that way in Deep Flying because you're towed down one-by-one, and courses and rules are laid out such that we can tell who rounds the turn points and who doesn't. But it was almost that freaky, because there the guy was, mopping up impressive finishes like...like he'd invented the sport.

Everyone began to take to him, too. I couldn't stand that. He was the life of the party, goofing off, drinking with anyone who'd buy, and the cork class guys ate that up. The Average Joe's hero, that was Brian. Even the established pilots toasted him. Everyone seems to be drawn to the happy-go-lucky type...everyone likes that. I liked it in Will, but then Will wasn't a big fake, pretending to be the uncomplicated fool, the man with no ill will and no agenda. And Will wasn't a reckless powder keg of calamity.

Brian never won an Open Distance meet that I recall. Most meets are a race to goal, with turn points and a finish line that's well defined. Very, very few just let you go as far as you want in any direction until you bob to the top. Those that do are either because conditions are poor, or because the meet officials lack the experience or equipment to set up or score more complex courses...or very rarely an Open Distance heat is just held to showcase the very best, like letting horses run free. Get big mileage numbers for the newspapers. Get a huge story. All out; anything goes. Like today.

Well, you want a story? I'm giving you a story.

CHAPTER TWELVE

I started out to tell stuff like how the Outer Banks meet went; I never dreamed this damned battery would hold up enough to let me get this far, to get this much of our history out. Looks like I've decided to keep going...I don't know, maybe I wanted to see if I have the nerve to share this next part. Been working up to it, I guess...wouldn't have come anywhere near it for the longest time, but...well the point is that I've blamed Brian for every foul thing that has ever happened to me. And now today, too...I went into today still thinking that, still feeling that.

Hell, it's never gonna stop haunting me unless I just tell this. I don't know any other way. Not easy, though...but it's part of the whole thing, and in fact defines so much of my own sentiments...well, this and the thing about my dad. Okay, just get it out. To my two little ones...I don't care if the rest of the world knows the details or not...but, um...Jeannie and Karina, this is what really happened:

It was in honor of my thirtieth birthday, although half a year in arrears. We'd been looking forward to the whole deal for months, making plans, paying deposits, coordinating schedules. It was supposed to be an epic week with Alan and Paul and their wives, and also Walt and Wendy Foxx, who were friends of Paul and new to our crowd. A real vacation for a change, everyone said, free of the pressures and scheduled itineraries of competition events—just sun and gentle breezes and carefree hours laughing and snapping pictures. Comparing it to the sport meet circuit, it would be more like a picnic instead of a timed overland trek.

There were some other moderately experienced mariners in this group, especially Paul, Steph and Alan, and I was looking forward to some relaxed sailing. Bob and Will were also good sailors but they couldn't make it. It was gonna be a change of pace in another way, too, since Deep Flying is so solitary by comparison. This trip was something we could share in real time with...with our, uh, wives.

I fully intended to let others man the little boat's helm while I enjoyed some cold beer and snoozes on deck. I wanted to get a mild sense of exploration in a new way, to anchor in private little coves and swim on little no-name beaches, and maybe do a little fishing off the stern when we were underway. I wasn't going to even glance at a chart.

We were pushing the season, given that we'd planned this at the tail end of the annual good weather...mostly because we could get a bit of a break on the prices. But everyone was optimistic, hoping for good luck; I imagined sunlit days, iced down Heinekens, fresh fish sizzling on deck-top grills...wives in bikinis...Eagles tunes sweeping down-breeze across the water. Adrienne was my love, my heart and my soul; and I pictured her kneeling behind me and smoothing sun cream on my shoulders while we leaned on each other's body. It was going to be the getaway of which memories were made.

The plan was laid out such that we'd all converge on a little lodge at Doe Bay the first night, getting there when and how we could. It was on Orcas Island in the San Juans, northwest of Seattle. A pretty little island, with rolling farmlands, a rugged coastline, marine and terrestrial and airborne wildlife—the very picture of peace and promise. Doe Bay was no more than a notch, an indent, an insignificant nick in the rocky perimeter of the island, but was famous locally nonetheless; it had a sheltered feel, and offered a little 'alternative' bunk house, pretty much like a hostel. The reason the lodge is there is that there's a natural hot springs with a swimsuits-optional tub, which meant that beautiful visitors felt compelled to go "au naturel" in the clear, steamy water, and locals felt compelled to come and gape at them.

We'd stashed our kids with Adrienne's parents, who adored them of course. Those were the first nights of their little lives they would spend away from us, but although we fully expected a tearful heart-rending goodbye, we had to chuckle at the way that whole scene went.

"You can play with Grandma and Grandpa all day until we get back," I said as I tousled Jeannie's hair, although what I meant was that they could play until they wore their grandparents to a frazzle.

"Yay!" was all I got in return. Her tone sounded suspiciously like, "Finally, somebody worth hangin' out with! Okay, beat it, Pops, don't let the screen door hit ya where the Good Lord split ya." But I took it like a man.

Adrienne knelt and gave them each a huge hug, smothering them with kisses and trying to maintain a brave face, hoping to dry her tears on their little shirts before they saw them rolling down her cheeks. Then she reached out and hugged both of them together, and I stepped in and gave the whole pile of them a big bear hug until they all squealed, even Mommy. Finally we stepped back and just smiled at the little ones, until three-year-old Karina looked up at me and said sweetly, "Daddy, you and Mommy can go now...you're going to be okay."

We laughed until we cried, squished them again for good measure, got another good squeal or two out of each, and then Adrienne hugged her parents and I thanked them, promising to call before we boarded the yacht and again after we docked her and were safely back on terra firma.

I'll never forget Adrienne's mom's anxious fidgeting, standing there on the doorstep...her lightly trembling fingers as she clutched first her daughter and then her daughter's kids, her quiet look of outer cheer and inner terror.

We drove straight to the airport and caught our plane a few hours later. Our connection took us through Dallas-Forth Worth. The air was bumpier over eastern Texas than I'd expected, given that it was mid-October. But it was warm down there for that time of year and had evidently rained a couple of days prior; the moisture in the air from the evaporation was still forming reasonably tall cumulus clouds in a layer over the fields below, like so many lumps of cotton all flat on the bottom and all floating at exactly the same height. Cumulus clouds have enormous power in them, especially the most extreme flavor, the Nimbus beasts; the updrafts can be unbelievable—it was even reported once long ago that some group of parachutists in France found themselves swept upward inside such a towering cloud at high velocity, into the icy air above, with most of them freezing to death as a result...and their chutes hadn't even been opened yet. Imagine air strong enough to reverse the direction of a two-hundred-pound falling man and rocket him skyward, into the realm of ice crystals. That's what I once heard, anyway. In my hang gliding years we called these updrafts "cloud suck" and avoided them like the bubonic, for fear of wings breaking off and ourselves plummeting thousands of feet in final horror. We always tried to find rising air, but not the kind of monster stuff you couldn't escape.

Anyway the plane just bumped along a bit, for an hour or so. The mountain states had more stable air, strangely, and I slept over most of them; Adrienne read the in-flight mag and a suspense novel she'd brought along.

In Seattle we disembarked and grabbed our rental car, heading up the coast to Anacortes, where we caught the evening ferry out to Orcas. From the dock there, it was only maybe twenty minutes and two map consultation stops to Doe Bay on the island's southeast side.

Paul and Steph were in the little cafe when we pulled up. They told us they'd been there a day already, killing a bit of time in some rental sea kayaks and such, and that Adrienne and I were the last of the party to arrive. Alan and Julia were just checking in, the Foxxes were in town picking up some pizza, having called an order in an hour earlier...and right about that time, with Adrienne looking at me in a strange and furtive way, I heard a bellow from the naked hot tub in the grove that made my blood boil.

This whole thing had originally been Adrienne's deal—she'd dreamed it up, had come up with the guest list from among our friends she thought were closest, had researched likely locations around the country and world that were within our budget, and had chosen my passion, sailing, as the main event. Clearly she'd done it all to ensure my ready agreement. In that instant, with that howl of stupidity still echoing on the rocks behind the hostel, I realized that her own agenda, her own birthday gift to me, was the hope of reconciliation between my estranged brother and myself.

My first reaction was to feel I'd been betrayed. The trip immediately went from exhilarating to ruined. I must have scowled instantly, and I stalked out without a word and alternately stomped and shuffled down to the shoreline, where I began to heave stones from the beach into the water by the handful. It didn't take me long to realize that if I behaved like that I'd ruin the thing for a lot of other people, all of whom had paid considerable money to be part of this, and all of whom clearly loved me as a friend and wanted to be part of an epic birthday week for me. I took more than one deep breath, sucked it up, and returned to the cafe with a bolted-on smile, declaring that I'd made a promise to my kids to waste no time throwing handfuls of stones into the water. It sounded like a stupid lie, and was, but I went with it, and after a moment they broke into grins and called me a strange one, blamed it on some rare strain of instant birthday-triggered dementia, and left it at that. Paul suggested we go soak up the hot springs warmth, but I begged off, claiming fatigue, and Adrienne showed her perceptiveness and loyalty by staying with me. "I don't want to break up the local couples by strutting my stuff," she joked. Paul said "dang" to that, and then Steph smacked him across the back of his head, and they laughed and graciously let us withdraw.

They brought a couple of pizza slices to our room later on. We turned in soon after, with a lot of quiet between us, and the last of the sun's light failed on the smooth water and pine trees around the little lodge, not long after it had failed on Cypress and Sinclair islands to the southeast.

None of this is easy to tell, here and now. For sake of my children I'll go on as long as I can. Looks like the battery is drooping a little more, but...maybe I can get it all out.

I awoke before everyone else and went for a long walk out the lane to the road and up the tree-lined grade. The sun was trying to stream low across the water and through the tall pines. The calm air seemed to promise a tranquil day, but the sky suggested already a bit of a breeze at very high altitudes. I knew the others would be stretching and yawning before too long, staggering over to the little cafe area to eat muesli or pastries, and I wanted to avoid for as long as I could the many pairs of eyes that would be watching my interaction with Lunfer. My only plan, and it was a poor one, was to bury the tension in energetic action on the boat, and just keep the one thing between us that worked best for me, which was distance.

I'd brought my camera for the morning hike, mostly as an excuse to be gone for a long time.

They picked me up two hours later on the way to the small docks on the island's southwest corner where we'd be renting the boat. I could tell they'd all been in on it—the guys had known since the day I'd admitted the family connection that I was ashamed of it, and Adrienne had told me more than once since that day in the coffee shop how disappointed she was in me, for being incapable of getting along with my own brother. Now in the car on the way to the boat, she and Alan tried to draw me out, but I remained quiet, claiming some kind of rapture over the scenery, particularly the mists over the open fields in the island's center. The others drove in Paul's rented van ahead of us. It was clear that by failing to greet him I'd made Lunfer feel unwelcome, because he was quiet and avoided me when we all got out. While we rode, Adrienne had softly asked me to make sure "everyone" felt a part of the group, and we both knew what she meant, but I also knew there were some things a guy cannot fake.

The yacht the man had reserved for us looked like a dream come true—a little two-masted Bermudan-ketch-rigged thing that had been born in Europe somewhere and had seen most of its service from Portland to Alaska...and, according to him, once from San Diego to the Tropic of Capricorn and back. How it had gotten across the Atlantic and then over to the North Pacific we could only guess. Stretching thirty eight feet from bow to stern, it had a steel hull, ample below-deck areas for sleeping and cooking, and an amazing, classic polished wheel made of New Zealand Kauri wood that made you want to do helm duty day and night. The boat was old, with steel stays holding up the masts that had seen quite a lot of duty, but we didn't expect to encounter any weather that would stress them. Our plan was just to ply the waters between the small archipelagos and maybe up the inside reaches near Vancouver Island's east side. Where it was sheltered, we'd said.

We signed and paid the deposit—a big wad of cash bills that the rental guy grabbed and caressed like a crystal ball—then set about readying the Fitful Mistress for the voyage. Part of this process was to demonstrate that we knew what we were about. Curtiss Delron, I think his name was...the man renting to us...he didn't know us; and he didn't own the yacht. He moored and maintained a little fleet of offerings, mostly smaller than this one, although all of them too big to trailer. That was his drawing card—a chance to sail something a person couldn't bring with them. The boats were owned by folks who didn't want them to float idle while they collected slip or mooring fees, which could break an owner in short order. This man had come up with a little business convincing owners to let him put their watercraft to profitable use, as long as he kept them seaworthy and ensured that the clients who sailed them did the same. I have no doubt that most of his clients were day-trippers, if nothing else judging by the relaxed approach he had to weather forecasts. He nodded and smiled while we checked and configured her, but he watched like a hawk, too, until he was convinced we knew the basics.

We left the sails furled for the time being, but set Stephanie and Wendy to removing and stowing the main sail's cover, so that we could raise the canvas once clear of land. Walt and Alan carried supplies aboard and stowed them below, occasionally choosing to leap across where the rail cable was left down near the stern rather than wait for each other at the short but narrow gangplank. Walt then parked the vehicles to the side of the little gravel lot, out of the way. Paul and I gathered together the charts that Delron had provided and studied them to be sure they covered all the water of interest. We noted they were old and were limited to sections within the sound, but Delron assured us that nature hadn't changed for several million years and that old charts would be just fine for our needs. Besides, they were all he had to offer. We put them in order according to our immediate interests and turned to inspecting nav equipment, the location of the ship-to-shore, and the engine, which we hoped to never need but considered a safety feature.

Alan checked out the running lights and the primary sail fittings, including pulleys, winches and cleats, and had turned to looking for some graphite or silicone spray to free up a couple of halyard shackles. In retrospect that and the dusty, sun-faded sail covers might have been a red flag to us that this boat hadn't been used or maintained in awhile, but no one thought of that at the time. Adrienne carefully went over the terms of the rental with Delron, our responsibilities regarding onboard systems like the head and the engine, and our timetable. She was new to big water sailing, but picked things up quickly and was very eager to help. And she made up for inexperience by applying common sense, reasoning that someone on shore ought to know our intentions, and that we should be aware of the most common headaches regarding geographic obstacles and other hazards. She also gave Delron the keys to both vehicles. She wrote everything down for him and for us.

Through all this, Brian stayed out of my way, and it was clear by his behavior and interaction with the group that he felt like the odd man out.

Fine by me; that's what he was. But I noticed he took a quick look at the charts after Paul and I had stowed them, and noted the gasoline level and read the placard over the engine start switch after I'd checked both, and generally followed my path around the boat, quietly and a few minutes behind me. I took it only to mean he had no clue what to do or what to check. He later quite expertly faked down the lines on deck, including the jib sheets, after testing the hand-crank winches, and I half-wondered how he knew to do those things. He also laid out the slack portions of the anchor line up on the bow, which I thought was stupid given that it would be hours before we'd ever need the anchor...but Delron made a comment about that, to the effect that there was a man who must have been in the Navy once and who knew on-deck safety. I scoffed inwardly but nodded a brief affirmation, hoping by some miracle that we'd put to sea and accidentally leave my brother on terra firma.

The boat was tied up bow-to-shore, starboard side against the dock. Wendy really wanted to cast off...and to yell "aye aye!" while doing so. Adrienne and Stephanie chimed in, and we made a big deal of it, with the three of them on the dock, Alan on the throttle, and myself, as team-designated Captain in honor of my birthday, at the helm. Curtiss Delron smiled, having seen this a hundred times but probably never with as much fun and flair as we did it. And I'm sure he didn't object to the sight of the girls in their halter tops, hair glistening in the late morning sun. I know we didn't, and to this day I remember.

Wendy started by taking a turn around the bollard with the bow line. I called to Steph to cast off the stern line, and she did, then stepped up amidships and bounded aboard. Next I asked Adrienne to disengage her beam line, toss it aboard, and take a position behind Wendy, both of them hauling on the line up there. Walt meanwhile pulled the two rear fenders aboard. Cutting the bow hard to starboard to kick the stern out, I asked Alan for forward throttle and he gave a brief burst, knowing I had no intention of ramming dry land. We sprung forward, levering against the bow bumper and limited by the bow line, and I immediately centered the rudder, called for full reverse engines, and then yelled, "Cast off bow line and come aboard!" Paul, Walt and Alan repeated the command in unison; Wendy and Adrienne whipped the hawser over the bollard and leaped off the dock for the deck, shouting "Aye aye, aye aye, aye aye!" for all they were worth. We were cracking up but making it work just the same. Brian positioned himself in the right place on the bow, and caught their arms as they came across, to steady them. I guessed he'd seen it in a movie somewhere.

So we sprung that thirty-eight-foot beauty off the dock like pros, not a motion wasted, not a false move made. Delron grinned and shook his head, and saluted me dramatically, and I returned it with an added wink. We were off, and all the world of water was ours to explore.

That first day we took it easy. Tide was ebbing and we were more focused on avoiding exposed rocks than on the skies. We motored slowly into the channel, noting shallow shoals to port early on, and the expected south-running current. Once there, I asked for engine idle. Alan cut the throttle and the thing died, but we didn't need it at the moment. He fiddled with it a few times while we drifted in the open water. Paul affixed the halyard to the mainsail's top shackle while Steph and Wendy removed the remaining ties that were still holding it to the boom. Alan abandoned the unneeded engine in favor of disengaging the boom's tether.

Using what little forward way we still had, I turned the bow into the light breeze. "Hoist 'er up," I said as dramatically as I could. I wanted to add a "shiver me timbers," but couldn't think how to work it in.

Paul looped the halyard under the cleat, dropped the bitter end, and hauled down repeatedly on it at the mast while Wendy fed the string of slides into the metal track. The sail went up, then got stuck in the slide track and they had to pull it down a ways to un-jam it. It was normal; we weren't concerned. It went all the way up after that, once Wendy figured out how to apply some downward tension to keep things straight, and the canvas luffed lightly in the breeze. I canted the rudder to let us catch some of it as we slowed and began a backward drift. The Mistress leaned over just a little once the sail scooped up the air, and Alan manned the boom line. Slowly we began to see a little wake behind the stern. We were underway.

Adrienne went around asking everyone where they'd like to berth. There were nine of us, and only enough comfortable mattresses below for six. Walt pointed out that someone would always be awake on watch, even when we were anchored at night, and I agreed; more than once I'd heard reports of anchors slipping and big boats destroying themselves against rugged shorelines—saw it once with my own eyes, in Villefranche-sur-Mer on the north Mediterranean coast—a small boat that broke her mooring—the owners weren't around and I marvelled at how the town allowed the beautiful little thing to drift shoreward over half a day's time and smash itself to splinters on the rocks.

Anyway, yes, we'd post a watch. Alan and I opted to roll out a mountaineering air mattress on the cabin floor and take turns using it between ourselves and Paul and Walt each night. I didn't once suggest that we'd give Brian watch duty; the thing was on my credit card, and I didn't want to hear drunken excuses as I stood witnessing a very expensive boat sink under my feet. Adrienne put Brian's sleeping berth forward under the forecastle area, in the sail locker. She didn't know it could be damp and smell like mildew up there. I think Brian found out soon enough. But he wasn't picky, I'll give him that.

The Fitful Mistress might have been fast enough, by the look of her, but we weren't trying that hard for speed, nor did we know her best sail set. Takes awhile to really get to know a ship. She had just a little more beam than the sleekest of boats, and I assumed she was designed somewhat for sleeping comfort on weekend jaunts and a homey feel on longer trips—not really for racing. But that suited us exactly. Paul joked that she was the only female he dared describe as beamy without risking his health, and Stephanie, who was proving to be an excellent husband whacker, cuffed him over the head with a fender, to the solemn approval of the rest of us, lest we incur the same treatment. I requested they stow those things below decks, as much to save Paul from a concussion as for any other reason, and while they were at it, haul out the life jackets and get everyone into one. We also went over the need to hang onto the stays whenever moving between cockpit and bow, and how to clip into the railing if things got bumpy. All the gear was old, including rail cables, so we mentioned that out loud too.

That first morning we puttered around West Sound for a little while, practicing tacking. I wanted to make sure everyone took turns manning the main's line before we pulled out the jib. The boat tacked alright under just the main if we had enough forward way and if I threw her into the turns, but she was surprisingly sluggish on jibes without the forward sail. I guessed it was because of her length, or her extra large keel, which you could feel. So anyway, when we all had the hang of it, I broke my silence with Lunfer to send him to the sail locker and look for the jib. Alan went with him, because we were pretty sure Brian wouldn't know a jib sail from a jock strap. They came back on deck a few minutes later with two large bags. One proved to hold a very moldy spinnaker, which we wanted no part of, and the other looked like a jib, so they shackled it up to the halyard, incrementally clipped its leading edge onto the bow stay, and began to unfurl.

It turned out to be much bigger than we wanted or needed. Because of all the exposed and subsurface hazards in those waters, I'd hoped to keep things simple and avoid rigging in ways that impeded visibility. This jib was big; it wrapped way back along the rail a lot farther than I was comfortable with. And there didn't appear to be another; I wasn't even sure it was the right sail for this boat. We unfurled it and tried it out; It caught on the main mast every time we swung the bow through the wind, and we needed someone up there to help it across. So we practiced for a good while, each crew member taking turns on the jib sheets and winches, poising for action when I'd call "Helm's A'lee," and then cranking like madmen when I followed with the standard yell of "Sheets!"

Wendy preferred to help in less physical ways, because she felt she was always underfoot when the scrambling began. She was my go-fer when I needed something from below. Adrienne really wanted to be in the thick of it, and got an intense look in her eye that I'll never forget. The winches took more frenzied arm strength than the girls had, though, especially since this crew had never sailed together and we were tripping over each others' feet in the cockpit area, meaning you had to be able to apply some fast muscle without bracing yourself in a good position for it. The guys were not having the easiest time of it, for that matter, lying across stuff and getting ankles stepped on while winching away. So Adrienne elected to be the one standing up on the bow to help the jib across. There was a bit of chop forming but the breeze was still moderate, so I didn't object. She seemed to have good balance and to be hanging onto the mast and stays. But I watched her.

We tried some jibes then, making sure we brought the main up short first and that everyone ducked when the boom swung through. And we did our best to ease that big timber across. I added a reminder about that to the normal command each time before I tossed the stern through the wind. We never messed with the mizzen mast at all; I knew nothing about how a boat handles with a mizzen sail set, and didn't see the point of complicating things. We were grateful for the added length of the boat compared to the available yawls and sloops Delron had, but we just did our best to keep it simple. We thought that would keep us safe.

By afternoon we felt we had a somewhat-better-than-landlubbers feel of the Mistress. The wind had strengthened for awhile, but then all but died. Something was changing up there. I could see the high clouds shifting shape. One small lenticular formed to the south, which meant the flow had gotten stronger way up above. Those were skies I'd have avoided with a hang glider.

I rounded the point and headed toward the mouth of East Sound, the larger bay created by Orcas Island's main lobes. My intention had been to sail there the second half of the first day, but we'd spent longer that expected in the smaller West Sound waters getting the sails set and practicing basic drills, and now the breeze had died. The slack tide was past and the water was on the rise again, which would help a little when it came, but we really didn't know what direction to expect of the currents in those channels. I opted to continue east with both sails set, following the ferry route for the time being, assuming it offered us fewer obstacles, excepting of course the ferries themselves.

So we angled east by southeast for awhile, passing...Blakely Island I think it was called...to port. Cameras came out when a small pod of porpoises surfaced nearby. I knew they were not Dall's because they didn't look like tiny killer whales. They had whitish sides, and hung together, so Julie decided they were something other than the numerous Harbor Porpoises common to shallow water out there.

It was slow going. Blakely...or Blake... whatever its name was...took us around forty minutes to pass. We got through the stretch between it and the island to the immediate south—Sinclair? Lopez?—I forget—anyway we got through just barely before having to veer off because of an oncoming ferry, which thankfully was easy to spot with its white color and tall profile and lights...and the fact that it took up half the narrow channel. The charts showed exposed rock hazards everywhere through here, yet there was very little visible that I could see, possibly because the tide was starting its flood phase, which almost made things dicier than if we'd seen the rocks. A rock puts just as big a crater in a hull when it's hiding below the surface.

After letting the ferry go by and taking its wake bow-first, we pointed east again and began to cross a far more exposed stretch of water, still angling to keep island terrain to port—this time Cypress Island. The new channel was deep and devoid of dangers, except that the chop was bigger and the current quite strong. The breeze picked up out here, from the south; amazing how the winds wrap around those islands like water around river boulders. We held a beam reach on the way across, and made better time, although hardly dunking any rails in the water as we went.

Walt and Wendy passed around some crackers and cheese to tide us over until dinner, since we'd all been distracted by our various duties. The snack mostly served to remind us that we were starving.

Finally had Guemas in sight. Day had turned to early evening, and I wanted to find somewhere to spend the night. As the boat traffic around that island was expected to be virtually nothing, it seemed like a good secluded neighborhood for a band of buccaneers such as we. I jibed us to port, almost running downwind, and pointed north by northwest, watching the Guemas shoreline carefully in this shallower, calmer stretch. The breeze weakened and our stomach rumbling strengthened as another hour went by. At last Paul spied a tiny bay with the binoculars that looked promising, and I jibed once more when I thought the moment was right and took her straight toward it.

It was a semicircular little cove no more than a hundred and fifty feet wide, with a little gravel beach made of smooth dark stones. The inlet, on the very northwest tip of the island, seemed sheltered enough. Trees hung down on either side and over some of the beach. They weren't quivering, so we could tell the air was quiet there, at least for the moment. Alan took bow lookout duty alongside Lunfer, who'd stayed up there most of the trip, at the opposite end of the boat from me. Alan called back that the approach looked clear, and once I'd provided an estimate of our exact location in the channel, Adrienne confirmed his assessment on the chart. We payed out the main line a little and continued in under wind power at a slow pace.

Everyone came on deck and paused to look. Walt and Paul suddenly expressed interest in exploring this strange little uninhabited world, and most of the others echoed that. I reminded them that we had no dingy, so whether we'd be able to get ashore or not depended on bottom contour or their willingness to freeze their asses off.

As we approached, we noted the steepness of the land above the waterline. It was maybe a twenty-degree slope right there, so it looked promising for getting the bow close to shore before the keel touched bottom. But to do that, we'd have to take it very slowly; I wasn't at all sure if this was how real yachtsmen would do it, and I didn't want any dents in the hull. We dropped the sails, stowed the jib in its bag, tied the main to the boom, and crept in at a snail's pace, gauging the sideways drift due to the whisper of breeze and current, sculling the rudder, and using an emergency paddle that Steph untied from the stern rail.

The bottom was gravel and mud here—no rocky obstacles visible in our immediate path. The closer we got, the less a factor the current became. We managed to get the bow nearly into ankle-deep water before the keel grounded gently against the mud.

Walt held the wheel steady while I went forward to take a look. Alan and I lowered ourselves off the bow pulpit into the water, carrying a line Paul had tied to the cleat. The water was cold. We waded ashore—a distance of only about thirty feet. We tied the line onto a pile of driftwood tree trunks that had been there for some time, then poked our heads briefly in through the wall of forest vegetation. What lay before us was a world covered by thick and bouncy mosses, a seemingly mythological place of cedars, ferns, mushrooms, and not a sign of human disturbance ever having occurred. It seemed like a little pocket of untouched Pacific Northwest, the way the entire region had probably once been and we guessed would never be again. We returned to below the boat's bow and helped the others climb down, except for Wendy, who wisely didn't want to get her clothing wet, and Brian, who wanted to fish and stayed back at the stern, needing the extra water depth that thirty eight feet of hull made reachable.

The water and air remained calm through all this. We were able to just keep the Fitful Mistress there with that one thin line and the keel squished lightly into the sloping mud bottom. I'd stepped off the boat simply to get my feet wet, so to speak, to see for myself what the bottom was made of, and to get that briefest glimpse of the forest beyond the front line of driftwood and trees. When the others were ashore I climbed back aboard to ensure it wasn't moving and to take another look at the tide tables, charts, and weather.

While they poked around on shore, Wendy decided to fire up the little propane grill on the forecastle deck. Brian actually caught three nice Cabazon on a feathery black marabou jig, hopping it up and down with a hand line on the bottom, back at the stern. He was pretty messy cleaning them, and the cockpit smelled like fish guts the rest of the evening, but when the others returned they made a joke of it and were glad to get the fresh grilled slabs of fish. Lot of meat on a good-sized Cabazon. Wendy got some garlic butter onto them on the grill, and they did smell good.

The aroma was better than a loud dinner bell; it wafted shoreward, and they all popped out of the greenery like so many watermelon seeds squirting out of the fruit, then splashing their way back and jostling each other for first right to climb up on deck. The noise they made would have put an end to the productive fishing if Brian hadn't already quit, but luckily we had enough. I made them each take an oath of loyalty to the ship and to their captain before they could get back on; and anyone who didn't know the secret pirate's password, which turned out to be "gimme a hand here, dammit," was banned from boarding.

Once everyone was back on deck, Alan, Paul and I backed the boat off shore a little, using the paddle and gaff hook to push backward against the bottom, and then we set anchor. And we did it in one shot, and without the engine. We eyeballed it, and then pushed back as hard as we could and dropped it where the chart confirmed we'd have clearance in a full circle, even when the tide changed and no matter which direction we might drift. It caught and dug in, to my satisfaction...although I was "captaining" partly on the basis of having experience with much smaller boats, which never had a real anchor, and partly on the lore Dad and I had read all those years ago. Still, it seemed to hold. We cleated the line and then I took a few rough sightings and made some mental estimates of distances to this rock and that point. I didn't write them down, but I had a fair idea, and I told the others to take a real good look, and that if any of them thought we were dragging the anchor during the night, they should wake me.

The sky faded out; not a lot of stars, since the high clouds had remained and a few more had rolled in from points south and west. We ate and drank like a marauding Norse horde, and elected to leave stereo systems off, instead listening to each other and the echoes of the Puget Sound night. I insisted we ration the beer and wine, not because we lacked for any but because I didn't want you-know-who to become a liability. Everyone had to have good judgment on a trip like this, although I know it was too much to wish for.

The gentle shaking of a single little tree branch toward the back of the beach first spurred Stephanie to declare the breeze was picking up. But as we stood quietly and looked more closely, we realized there was a small deer eating leaves from that tree. It had no antlers, so must have been a doe, probably a blacktailed. Deer populate that whole archipelago, swimming out from the mainland and from one island to another as their whim strikes them, their predators force them, or their food supply requires. Guemas island was probably a good choice, given the complete absence of people, and I wondered how many of them might be there. There was high country on this island and a lot of protected places to hide, so I guessed there were probably small herds.

Not many people know that deer hair—all species, and including moose, elk and caribou—is hollow. So is antelope and horse hair, for that matter. It can float an animal like a cork, and they can cross great distances and sometimes survive even being swept out to sea by currents they didn't expect, as long as they find terra firma before hypothermia or meat eaters come along.

We cleaned the grill and stowed it. Jackets came out after that, as the air had turned chilly...and Walt's harmonica. We stayed on deck for a long while. At some point it got really dark, and down behind the jib lines piled near a winch, Julie found some fish parts that were still lending their aromatic loveliness to the night air. She picked them up gingerly and tossed them overboard, then suddenly let out a shout.

"Hey...did you see that?" she blurted over her shoulder to the rest of us.

"What?!" Wendy responded, leaping to her feet fast enough to rock the boat, by her tone probably assuming some carnivorous denizen circling the boat.

"Watch," Julie said. She tossed the last fish spine into the water while the boat tipped slightly, because by this time we were all standing at the rail. The widening concentric circles made by the little splash glistened an eerie fluorescent green as they spread, revealing the presence in the water of glowing diatoms that create light when disturbed. The effect was more magical than anything we could have expected, there in the quiet night of a strange and indifferent Eden. Then Paul took the boat hook, extended it down, and stirred the water with its tip; a swirl of bright green light followed his stroke and lingered for a second or more before fading. We began to take turns roiling and streaking the glassy liquid with the hook, the paddle, the end of a line...us guys spitting...anything to be charmed again and again by that divine little mystery. Those cold, oxygenated waters claim such diverse wonders of the miracle of life.

They claim life...there's an interesting phrase.

The moon remained hidden behind the high layer of clouds, but let its misty white soak through to us, as though spilling paint on the reverse side of a porous canvas. What I thought was a light catabatic breeze began a little after midnight or so. I know in hindsight that the weather was changing somewhat during the night. The Mistress drifted northwest gently to the end of her anchor line, but showed no signs of going anywhere beyond the intended range of her tether. We turned in below; Paul took first watch since he said he wasn't sleepy, and he awoke Alan a couple of hours later. Alan, ever the trooper, didn't wake me until just before sunrise. We sat for a few minutes on the forecastle deck, me still wrapped in a sleeping bag, speculating on the increased cloud cover and the feel of the breeze.

On the beach just before dawn, atop a driftwood tree trunk that protruded one thick branch into the air, we saw a sea otter straining its sleek neck to get a better look at who and what we were.

Adrienne came up on deck and we shared the sleeping bag like a big blanket. When Alan went aft, she broached the subject we'd not discussed on the trip up to now. She said to me gently that estrangement was no way for brothers to go through life, and that she'd invited Lunfer thinking it a good way to spend time away from present cares and past haunts...past ghosts. She asked me to try to start anew. She'd always made excuses for me, believed the best and all that, and had maintained that all we needed was to get away from prior bad luck and see each other as human beings.

And she'd always seen good in Brian too. She used to say that despite his outward irresponsible abandon, he was a broken man, bent on atonement but not knowing it. She believed he was carrying the load not only of my parents but of his too. She thought he looked up to me and wanted to have a family but didn't know how to hold onto it.

Lunfer liked her, too, which was no surprise because she saw qualities in him that weren't there, not that I saw anyway. That's what women do for men, and miraculously those very qualities then sometimes grow. The fact that he cared for her was one reason why I never tried to associate any of us with him. I didn't want my children to emulate or gravitate toward that trashy kind of attitude. Didn't want "Uncle Brian" to corrupt them; didn't want his influence in our lives at all. I wanted to leave that whole bad mistake my parents had made behind, to undo an error that had been committed long before. I knew it was my job to protect my children.

She kissed me, there on the deck in the early light a little after dawn, and asked me to vow that I'd give it my very best effort. I looked into her eyes, but I just couldn't make that promise.

CHAPTER THIRTEEN

I could hear the others beginning to move below deck, yawning, laughing, stowing the sleeping berths. Someone started a pillow fight and then declared a boat fender an illegal weapon; another seconded the sentiment for socks and underwear. After twenty minutes or so they slid back the hatch and came tumbling out into the morning air with steaming coffee mugs in hand. Julie brought two forward for Adrienne and me, and we grabbed them eagerly and sipped, until Paul called to me from the cockpit that he thought the anchor had dragged just a bit over the night. I stood up and took some rough sightings to the points on land nearest us. Hard to tell, since the tide was different and we'd swung to a different point of the circle from where I'd had a look the night before, but it didn't matter much because we were awake now, we hadn't drifted into any real danger yet, and the breeze at the moment was swinging us out, away from Guemas' rocks.

Still, we had to weigh anchor before getting underway. We made sure everyone was awake and dressed, the coffee mugs were stowed, and there was general agreement that we had a crew who was ready to sail. We pulled out the warm clothing because of the chill in the air and the way the sky looked, and pored over the charts anew, to refresh our memories of the headings and hazards. We'd sail north and west, in hopes of seeing something interesting around the Gulf Island Marine Reserve, in Canadian waters, and maybe put in somewhere nondescript on what we assumed would be the leeward side of that monstrous weather-shielding mountain range known as Vancouver Island. Alan took great delight in hyping up the fact that we had no passports on us, or permissions to land, and that the moment we touched toe to Canadian gravel we'd be nothing less than invaders.

When everything was battened down and all was ready, Alan took the helm while Paul and I stood on the bow, pulling carefully in unison on the anchor line, maintaining a half turn around the deck cleat as we did so. Since we'd not bothered to check the engine that morning and had assumed it was still unreliable, we took this process very slowly; we didn't want to overshoot the anchor's position due to excess momentum, drift shoreward, and run aground. The bow crept over the spot; the anchor wasn't budging. I jumped a couple of times, pitching the bow up and down, while Paul captured the slack with the cleat on each successive downward pitch. It took only about three good cycles for the buoyancy of the hull to spring the anchor out of the mud below.

For the moment we were completely still, with the bow still pointed into the very light breeze, but we weren't very far from the little gravel beach. Adrienne, Brian and Steph had partly unfurled the main sail and were readying to manipulate the boom whichever way Alan needed. He asked for a little more pull on the halyard to get some extra canvas in the air, and while Walt obliged, Alan cut the helm hard to starboard and asked them to swing the main's boom out to the same side and hold it there. It didn't work as well as a jib might have—not as quickly anyway—but the Mistress backed down ever so slowly, away from the cove, and her bow fell off to where the wind was to starboard. We centered the boom and let the turn continue, and then suddenly we were on a broad reach, and then running nearly downwind. I yelled "Jibe Ho" for Alan, since he'd taken a bite of an orange right then and couldn't, and added "look out for the damn boom," because they'd not rigged her in and she came very close to knocking Stephanie over the side. Brian lunged for the boom itself and tried to pit his muscle against a few tons of breeze, when he should have grabbed its mainsheet. Steph grabbed a stay at the last second and hung on. It was lucky that the wind was still so gentle. We should have learned from it.

We went around the top end of Cypress Island and looked north. Much bigger water out there, from that vantage point, and the chart agreed, but we also thought it would probably be more clear of exposed hazards, due to the depth. A harbor seal resembling nothing so much as a large brown puppy dog surfaced off our port bow, and studied us carefully with voluminous, dark, disturbingly clairvoyant eyes.

I think it was around nine o'clock by then. The weather was already deteriorating. We set a course and began the big water crossing. The wind was from behind us, and we were more or less running with it, which meant we couldn't make really great time. Just consistent progress. I tried to get us on a reach a few times, but although the speeds through the water increased a little, I decided it wouldn't make up for the extra distance we'd have to go by doing it. The currents were strange—strong and then backwater-ish, then strong again, with alternate chop and upwelling, and forming shear lines like river eddies, or like air does on a cloud street's edge. The day took on an ominous chill, and the sky began to spit at us a little here and there, as if to suggest we weren't welcome out in that stretch. But otherwise the long downwind leg was like a period of calm before all hell broke loose.

I took the helm again, while Alan and Paul tried to get the engine started. She'd roar and then die, or else idle and then die. I said it sounded flooded and Paul disagreed, saying it had to be starved. They tried to chase down whether there was a kink or bubble in the fuel line, or maybe a clogged filter, or whether it might be something electrical, which is always a prime suspect with an engine—whether spark plug wires were loose or shorting against anything wet or metal—but the effort wasn't yielding an answer. My vote was for fuel starvation because a couple of times it ran for several minutes, and we thought they had it, but it didn't last. Not long enough to rely on, anyway. And we were afraid we'd drain what was left of the battery, which by the look of it was one of the first power cells ever manufactured by Neanderthal man.

All of this took an hour, maybe two. We jibed and took the long shoreline of Lummi Island to starboard, but a long way off, on a broad reach. We were still in US waters, but I knew the border was an imaginary line drawn on the Sound's surface about twelve to fifteen miles northwest of our position. Paul took another very long look at the worsening sky, calling my attention to a squall line that had set up to the southeast. He didn't like the idea of going on to the Gulf Islands Reserve in one shot, arguing that a safe port and hot coffee sounded a lot better. "This is our vacation, not some blood and guts expedition," he said, or something to that effect.

But we couldn't spot a safe place to put in that was in easy reach, or couldn't agree, I forget which. Some of both, I guess. At some point the south wind abruptly turned southeast, and strengthened to twenty knots or better. I didn't know whether that was because of our new position—maybe we'd crossed a shear line—or because things were changing, like the sky was coming undone. But either way it was threatening to push us way up through the big expanse of exposed water that constitutes the open mouth of the famed Inside Passage. I can tell you that to novice sailors in a thirty-eight-foot tub, it doesn't seem so "inside." The choppy waves began to get much bigger; and they were following seas, which meant they came upon us from the stern. They hit us port stern first; every wave rolled and pitched and spun us wildly, and that began to make the boom plunge around, and made it hard to hold a heading.

And to make good on the nasty promise the spitting sky had vocalized earlier, now it began to rain. We scurried to get the charts below, and everyone dug for foul weather gear, which I realized was something we should have done long before when the sweaters and jackets had come out. Half of us were pretty drenched before everybody got buttoned up. Adrienne...she got me mine before she took care of herself. Visibility went to hell, and while they were scrambling I shouted for someone to get up on the bow, and Brian went up there. I didn't trust his judgment or his ability to communicate, and when Adrienne finished buttoning up my rain gear, like a fool I asked her to go forward partway so that she could relay anything back to me that he might call out. And in general, if he was keeping an eye out for the sake of the boat, then we needed someone to keep an eye on him.

Wendy, Walt, Julie and Steph went below pretty quickly, to keep from getting chilled to the bone more than they already were. Now they were getting seasick down there, from all the triple-axis tossing around. Below decks is the worst, because your eyes can't find a stable frame of reference. Myself, I couldn't see a thing, and couldn't hear anything from Brian or Adrienne. The so-called vacation had turned from controlled to hellish in a very short time.

I guess I'd waited too long; now there was no way I was going to steer toward shore in these squalls, not with all the exposed rock and reef hazards we'd seen up to that point, and not without knowing how far a given squall extended. We should have been paying attention to the radio. Like idiots we hadn't even familiarized ourselves with how to operate the ship-to-shore yet; we only knew on which bulkhead it hung. At this point our best bet seemed to be to continue north in open water and hope to outrun or outlast this squall.

I think we completely overshot the Gulf Islands, by the few sightings I could manage, and by what we were told later. We must have been almost even with the northern Galiano strand. That's way up there...combination of wind and currents. And we still lacked the maneuverability an engine would have given us, which was another reason I dared not take us any closer to a shoreline or try to get into an inlet or port. Age-old sailing lore, which was what I was riding on instead of the experience my friends thought I had, said that open water was our safest option, our only guarantee against running aground and losing the boat and possibly ourselves. If I had that decision to make again, I'd ram the first damn bit of shoal with all I had and make us cling there en masse, or swim for it.

The following seas got bigger. A second component of shorter, choppier waves, crossing from south-southwest and hitting us broadside, made the boat rock violently. Might have been caused by some other, larger craft, but I couldn't see or hear anything. We needed the sail to maintain control and try to get past the squall, so we couldn't just center it and crank it down. And the line must have somehow come off the cleat. With half the crew below and no one to tend it, the boom swung wildly back and forth as the seas rocked us, thudding against the mast stays with a sound I knew was loud but couldn't hear over the wind. I think that's when it must have happened. I couldn't see a thing now to port, where I was trying to sight our position. Alan grabbed Brian and wanted to reef the main sail, to reduce its area while still leaving some of it up, but I stopped them. "Get me Adrienne," I shouted to Lunfer.

He went forward, gripping the stays to keep balance as he staggered along the rail, up to where he and she had supposedly been doing bow lookout. I lost sight of him behind the sail.

He was up there more than a few minutes and I turned to Paul, to discuss in shouting tones whether shelter might still be our best bet after all. Rain continued to pelt our faces, making conversation difficult.

I turned to look at our wake and what little of the sky I could make out behind us, studying it for a few minutes but learning virtually nothing. When I looked forward again, I caught a glimpse of Lunfer down below decks. He appeared to be goofing off, sightseeing out the small round portals. I called to Adrienne, hoping to get her to poke her head out of the cabin long enough to add her opinion to Paul's, whose vote was still to brave a landing somewhere. She didn't respond, and I hollered at Lunfer to get her attention for me. He came out on deck and started to stumble forward again.

"What are you doing?" I yelled. "Can you get Adrienne?"

He nodded but kept going forward, disappearing under and behind the main sail. Paul said he'd get her, and started forward.

"No, isn't she below? Didn't Lunfer bring her back a few minutes ago?"

"She's not down there," Paul shouted in reply, looking in through the cabin's aft window. "He never brought her back that I saw!" And he continued on forward. A moment later he reappeared from behind the mast and shrugged.

"Lunfer!" I screamed...then, "Somebody check the head!"

By this time Julie caught what we were doing and checked, but found both the head and the sail locker empty. When you run out of places on a boat, it's bad.

"Lunfer!" I was in instant panic.

He took his time coming aft, looking all around, and tried to slip into the cabin again without looking me in the eye.

"Where the hell are you going?!" I hollered over the wind. "I told you to go get Adrienne! Did you? What did she say? Where is she?"

"I went up there, but couldn't find her."

"What do you mean?! Where is she?!"

"I wuz, uh...lookin'...." was all he could say.

It was unthinkable, and I turned frantic. The first thing I did was grab anything I could get my hands on around me and chuck it overboard, including my life vest, my jacket and the chart I'd tucked under it, and I don't know what else. All their faces went blank while I did this, but the part of my brain that formulates words had gone dead. Then I threw the wheel into the most violent turn I could make, not even bothering to call to anyone else to watch their heads. The boom swung center like a reaping machine as we came about and pointed close to the wind.

Alan was the first to figure out what I was up to. He leaped below and grabbed the fenders we'd stowed the day before at the dock, and heaved them overboard, and followed them with one of the two life rings. "Man overboard, man overboard, man...uh, Adrienne might have fallen overboard!" he repeated, until the others caught on. He ripped off his jacket, but Paul stopped him before he heaved it in. "Might need some for later," Paul advised.

They all saw it then, as they looked at the stuff in the water drifting past us. Markers. We had no engine. When you look for someone and you're under sail, you pretty much have to do long oval loops in multiple passes, tacking or jibing at each end. How do you know where you've been...the point beyond which your swimmer cannot be? Floating debris can make all the difference.

They got out on deck, every one of them, but it was still impossible to see. The driving rain wasn't letting up; we were probably in the worst of the squall at that moment, or that's the way I remember it anyway. I was beyond madness already; Paul took the helm while I leaped from rail to rail, looking, shouting. For an instant I even tried to shinny up the mast, thinking I might be able to get a better view—like a Crow's Nest—but a smooth, glossy, wet pole is not something that can be climbed by a lunatic. Julie did another check of the below-deck areas, I think more to keep me in hope than out of any chance we'd missed seeing my wife down there. How far back to sail? Lunfer would be of no use...probably hadn't even been paying attention...and with the main's canvas blocking our view, none of the rest of us had seen Adrienne for some time; she was supposed to be on the bow, with that reckless asshole!

You can't imagine how hard it is to, uh, relive those moments now, those initial, interminable moments of...of uncertainty. It's not...it's not...but, um...okay...but it was worse then, that first feeling, than in the, uh, telling. Okay, okay....

I remember...that, um...that I kept recalling the swing...and thud...of the boom, some minutes before, while still knowing that that recollection could be more misleading than helpful. There'd been a lot of wild rocking, and she'd clearly not been clipped into the rail. But we had little else to go on. There was no way to know how to sail back to exactly the same water we'd come through, either, because the current was still strong and still varied, place to place. We could only guess, and I called the turns while Paul made them and Alan and Walt did their best to give him sail settings that did some good. I reasoned that if we were drifting north on each pass, and we were, then Adrienne would probably be too.

We needed to find her in less time than it would have taken to make a radio call, let alone waiting for help. It was all on us, and I knew that. Ten minutes went by. Ten more. Jibe! No no no no, keep going straight, see the stuff on the water?! Five more. Tack, and more toward that angle there! Did she have her life jacket buckled up?! Was it over her raincoat or underneath?! Someone said at one point she'd removed it to zip up her raincoat better...did she put it back on? I realized we should never have included life vests in the flotsam we'd thrown into the water, because now I couldn't tell if hers was missing or not. Adriennnnnnnnnnnnnnne!

Paul found a hand-held air horn with some pressure still left in it, in the back of a gear locker down below, and was blasting it in all directions, hoping to see a raised arm in reply, somewhere in the chop and whitecaps. Fifteen more minutes. Some of the others were by now wondering what else they could do...and the situation was all beginning to sink in. In deliberate denial, I was still peering into the rain, shouting, crying out her name. I imagined Adrienne hearing it and waving us down, or swimming toward us. Not likely, you say, given the cold water and the time that had already passed, but what else was there to cling to? I was thinking about just how clumsy we were in maneuvering that boat, when Walt came back from the bow with a face as white as the sail.

"What?!" I demanded, as if anything could get worse.

"Brian isn't on the boat."

"What?!"

"Not on the bow, I just went up there! Not below."

Alan said we'd seen him last right after we figured out Adrienne was gone. "When you turned back upwind the second time, and the sail started to luff, did anyone see him up there?" he asked. "I didn't. Was anyone on the bow?"

"If he fell in at that point, he'll be downwind of our loops!" Paul pointed out.

I could see where they were going with this, and it wasn't gonna happen. "We're not!" I seethed. "We're not going down there to find that prick! Adrienne is somewhere way up here! She could be twenty minutes' distance upwind of that! She needs us to find her!" And I leaped back and began to wrestle Paul for the ship's wheel, trying to throw it into another upwind run.

Paul let me have it, too. He took a step back. Nobody knew what to say. We were suddenly faced with a choice of who to look for...who to save. Every second was a matter of life and death to someone in this water...might go numb in twenty or thirty minutes, or even less, no longer able to tread water or hang onto whatever they might be clinging to. No longer able to breathe. None of them had the heart to ask me to call off or postpone our search for Adrienne, even to go find someone whose location was a lot easier to estimate and who'd been in the water a fraction of the time. And they surprised themselves, too, because faced with a choice, they each realized that their confusion had begun to get the better of their hope. They were no longer wondering where and when we'd recover Adrienne, but if.

I took us further upwind than any of the other passes, maybe because I thought that that's where she'd be, maybe partly as a statement that I was the goddamn captain and I didn't care if Lunfer drowned as long as I got my children's mother back. All would be well if we only lost one, and if it was the one nobody would care about anyway. That sort of thing. I took us upwind, then north, mid-channel, and kept going, maybe a couple of miles.

"Nolan," Paul said softly.

"No! Shut up!" Hot tears were streaming down my cheeks.

Stephanie stepped up and touched me on the arm. I cried audibly now—couldn't stop it anymore—and Paul gently took the wheel, saying, "Let's cross the channel here...we haven't looked here, I'm sure of it. Everybody on the rail, everybody look for Adrienne! Steph, here, use the air horn if you see anything! This has gotta be the place!"

My knees went weak. They propped me up along the rail with them and we all peered into the choppy waves and the rain, which was finally letting up just a hair, although not nearly enough. We looked and looked, on both sides, now and then one of them exclaiming, but then always saying no, never mind. We all knew this was our last good pass. Julie ventured that Adrienne might have drifted toward a rock or shoal and we'd find her after the storm—the innocence talking, the fictional stuff we get from living pampered, safe, quiet, urban lives.

Alan and Paul began to calculate softly to themselves, and I knew what they were doing, but there was no fight left in me and nothing I could say. They were reasoning where a swimmer like Lunfer might be if way downwind. No one looked at me; they kept their eyes glued to the water. They did ask me twice if I wanted this pass to maintain heading or not, but I no longer had an opinion that could outbid alternatives. I just held my breath, looked for her face, cried, and prayed.

It took an hour to find Lunfer. He wasn't moving, but because of his life jacket, he was still afloat. His head was a small round dot, hard to see even when the water went momentarily smooth. It was blind luck that Wendy had spotted him. They steered the Mistress to approach him in a slow drift, and when we got close enough Steph threw him the one life ring we still had on board. It had a line attached to it, and she made a terrific throw, but he couldn't even grab for the thing. But his head did turn a little to look. Paul passed him with the boat and then came about, and expertly drifted down broadside on him, and Alan lunged repeatedly with the boat hook and caught a strap of his life vest on the fifth or sixth try. Then they guided him back toward the stern, and both Alan and Walt had to get into the water to help heave him up. Took them all to drag him aboard. His stare was no more or less vacant than it ever was. I didn't help; I kept looking for the one I wanted to find, hating him for needlessly complicating and cancelling the search for Adrienne, for managing to grab center stage once again, for the fact that we hadn't found her. I told myself we would have; I resented that everyone else had managed to stay on board but that he'd found a way to do the worst thing imaginable, just to get attention, in the process once again ensuring failure and calamity and the ruination of my life. No, I didn't help them pull him up; instead I went to the bow and furtively searched the waves, thinking I'd spot Adrienne here, reasoning quite stupidly, per the rule of happy endings, that she must be here too.

Lunfer was in a bad way; they force-fed him warm tea, got his feet into hot water, and now that some delayed assistance might actually mean something, Alan managed to figure out the ship-to-shore and get someone on the other end, telling them our situation. The wind had abated to thirty or forty percent of what it had been, although still as high as twenty knots by the feel of the worst of the gusts, and there was still rain, and current; we still could see very little and still were being swept north. With the engine situation what it was, they knew we could flounder around out there for hours trying to figure out where we were and trying to find a port where there might be a doctor for Lunfer.

Alan then went back to trying to fire up the engine, which still only ran until revved past idle. Useless.

A coast guard forty-footer out of Bellingham found us thirty five minutes later—it must have been in the channel on patrol already when they got the call. They tossed us a line and towed us to their home port, after two of them came aboard with basic medical stuff to hear our story and take control. They didn't say much, and one of them attended to Lunfer, who was now shivering uncontrollably, and that was supposed to be an improvement, a good sign. I searched the other's eyes for indications that they'd picked up a swimmer or had heard of someone who had, but I dared not ask outright, because I wanted to keep my last dim hopes alive. I saw them speaking with Alan and Paul in low, serious tones, and there were no looks of ecstatic relief.

I don't know how long the tow into Bellingham took. Another hour or even more. We crossed the channel and I pictured my wife everywhere, on every breaking wave crest and in every trough. The others dropped the sail entirely and eventually retired to the cabin, down to where Lunfer was slowly coming around. I alone stayed out on deck, drenched to the bone, up near the bow. I remember it was dusk when we were pulled alongside the dock.

They tied the Mistress up and herded us off, into a waiting van, and Lunfer into another, to take him to get checked out. He was walking almost as well as I was. They brought the rest of us in and got all our statements, took our IDs, filled out reports. I told them I didn't want to waste time on that, I wanted to get back out there, but they only said there were other people for that. Alerts had already been issued. They tried to commiserate—wasn't our fault, things can get dicey out there, gusts around Bellingham had topped fifty miles per hour and lots of folks were without power, etc. Something about a tropical storm way south in the Pacific causing instability, upsetting patterns around the eastern rim. They commented that the weather was slackening and that this could help, but declined to answer my questions whether the current conditions would stop people from beginning the search immediately.

They asked a lot of useless questions too— why hadn't we checked for advisories? Had the yacht rental guy warned us of approaching weather? Had I been drinking? Was my wife wearing a life vest, or if not, then why not? Did we see her fall in? Why didn't we call for help immediately? ...and all I could say was that we were panicked and in denial—and that by the time we realized there was a problem, we were all there was...the cavalry would already have been too late. They didn't deny that, either.

And they asked why Lunfer ended up in the water. Why was he the only one on board without a spouse? Who was he to me? Their focus seemed to be on finding fault rather than on saving the day, and I realized that we may be in port but that saving the day was still up to me.

Except for Lunfer, who stayed in their infirmary for observation, they took us to a cheap motel on the front street, where the Coast Guard and Sheriff's department could get ready access to us for information they might need. They put the couples in their own rooms and me in my own, and brought food, asked a few more questions, advised us to stay put, and left in what had slackened to a light drizzle.

I collapsed on the bed without bothering to take off my coat and wet clothing, only half believing they were out there looking. I must have sunk into a disturbed, fitful sleep. Around one in the morning I awoke with a start, the memory of an image fresh in my mind. I'd seen Adrienne...I'd had a premonition of where she was! I saw a soggy driftwood log near a rocky point, and her head on its opposite side, long brown hair draped over the wet wood in my direction...and what looked like fingers atop it, where she clung to it. She had washed up just outside the motel! Leaping to my feet, I threw open the door and bolted out into the damp drizzle, running at full tilt down the street to an empty lot that fronted the shoreline. I slipped and hit the pavement but it didn't even slow me down. I saw that a few rocks formed a kind of point off to the right, exactly like I'd seen in the vision; I knew she would be just beyond them. I waded out, but saw nothing. Waist deep water gave way to chest deep, then more. I swam out, shouting for her. It was dark, the only light leaking weakly from a street lamp on the road out past the empty lot behind me. I knew I had to strain my eyes and get out further, away from the artificial glare. Flailing and treading, I made it around the bend, then swept back to the left, shouting, pleading. The memory of my vision began to fade, and I fought to hang onto it, imagining that she'd fixed one eye on me above the log, beckoning me to come and find her there, right there.

I must have been out there the better part of twenty minutes at that point. I was in deep water now, and convulsing uncontrollably from the exertion and cold; I'd already begun to lose the ability to swim. My voice got weaker and I breathed a lungful of water once or twice, coughing, burning critical energy to fight my way back to the surface. Still couldn't get to her.

You'd think that a hand on your shoulder would make you jump out of your skin, but not if you're so completely spent there's nothing left for reaction. The black neoprene suit bumped against me and a man tipped me on my back and towed me toward shore, one arm across my chest to my armpit. I tried to fight, to make him understand that she was right there somewhere, just out past where I was...on a log...but he was far stronger than me, and I could barely gurgle a few senseless words.

And...that was it...that was all. That was the end of Adrienne. My wife, my love, the mother of my children...uh...was, um, gone...in the blink of an eye...in a week that she'd planned as a gift to me. No one ever found her. They said I'd been hallucinating out of grief and fatigue, and even I couldn't argue with them, as the vivid recollection of the premonition I'd seen was a memory I could no longer access in my mind. It had evaporated, like she had.

...Karina...Jeanne...I'm so....

I...uh...guess I was purple and blue after the rescue swimmer pulled me out. Someone had evidently heard me hollering, or had seen me go in. There was a warehouse near the empty lot, and it might have been a security guard there. Doesn't matter. The wetsuit guy was a cop; some other cops were there too, and tried to console me, to dismiss my vision as meaningless, saying that people in shock are often torn between hallucinations of finding their loved ones and ending it all themselves. Goes to show how much of what so-called experts say is made up. I might have had a fever, but no death wish. Although I could no longer picture it, I knew what my words had said I'd seen; I kept saying to them I'd seen her there, looking at me with one eye over the log, trying to raise her head.

They took me to the hospital and pumped warm liquids into me, stitched up the bloody gash I'd gotten when I'd fallen on the pavement, and probably sedated me until I drifted off—a mercy move to spare me any more hallucinations, I guess. By my own experience the night before—the fact that I'd lost the ability to tread water in so short a time—I realized at some point that Adrienne hadn't even lasted as long as it took us to pull Lunfer aboard, and maybe far less yet. It had been probably two hours or more at the point we'd found him, from when she'd fallen. I pray to God she hit her head on the boat and spared herself the knowledge that it was the end. If not, and if she'd gone in without her life vest...and we'll never know...she'd have been drowned long before Lunfer was back on board. We may have passed right over her as she sank, as she looked up to see our sleek, pretty hull slide on by and fade...as she'd waved a final weak farewell to me, from down in that dim, cold, watery grave.

The story hit national news, as you'd expect. Everyone delights in a gripping human drama. Adrienne's parents were out there standing in front of my hospital bed within nine hours...but the full finality had already hit me. I couldn't say a word to them...couldn't even look at them. I lay curled in a tight ball, fingers clenching my ankles until the nails made hamburger of my skin and they had to tape gauze to my hands. I was so empty with shame and anguish I couldn't apologize to them, couldn't cry or move or breathe, or even gag. I was a dead body that still had a pulse.

And hatred. That part wouldn't go away.

CHAPTER FOURTEEN

As I said, I couldn't have told that account to anyone for some years...telling something means you're reliving it, and it's slashed in deep gouges of pain on my soul as it is. But maybe it's good to talk about it; they always say that. I know I couldn't have done it to someone's face, but to a pod wall and a voice recorder control panel...I guess it was different. So anyway, if you're hearing all this, now you know.

It took me many months even to say her name; every time the little ones cried for their Mommy I'd all but break down and have to go outside, kick something, take some deep breaths, distract myself. I've been selfish...that reaction didn't help them very much. I love my kids and I hug them as much as any Dad ever did, and if there's a silver lining it's that we've become very close since we lost

Adrienne...although those consolation prizes Life serves up never erase the horrible defeats.

It's just that I've felt so...helpless. I'm adept, by nature—a problem solver—and yet I couldn't fix the thing that mattered. Couldn't face it. Could only place blame, and privately fan that wild flame of contempt.

It didn't help that there was an investigation that went on for a long time, and that it seemed to center on me. The Feds got involved. There were countless...interviews, they called them, although I knew them to be the interrogations they really were. They knew there's been no love lost between me and Brian, and the fact that he too almost bit the dust on the sailing trip made them suspicious. They questioned my decisions a hundred different ways, made me get psych tests...the whole bit. They never said they thought a crime was committed and they never stated that I was a suspect, but I could tell they were hoping to find something that would turn me into one. I guess to those who love to police the world, evidence of dastardly deeds is good news.

They bought Brian's whole gig right off—the lumbering, good-natured bear of a man, socially and intellectually challenged but loyal to the end...not a negative bone in his body.... The national papers and news channels got hold of something one of the Bellingham police had said, and it caught like fire. The guy had speculated, after having spoken with Lunfer in the infirmary, that Brian might have been "testing drift directions and running current strength suppositions through his head" as he was out there treading water. Where he got that we'll never know, because even I doubted that Brian had been articulate enough to hint at such an assertion...but somehow the cop drew that conclusion. It was the kind of thing the public is always dying to hear—like, I don't know, some tale about a loyal dog riding in a search helicopter who spots his master, chews the leash off, and leaps a hundred feet into the raging river to pull the unconscious man to shore inches above the falls. People always eat that kind of thing up, even if it's obviously fiction. Feel-good stories are just that, and nobody really wants to discern. So Brian was suddenly the selfless giant, the simpleton above pettiness and above reproach. He became an instant hero. I imagined him milking that for all it was worth, scoring hundreds of rounds of beers in every pub at every Deep Flying meet from here to Anchorage...boasting, strutting, soaking it up...catapulting his life to the stratosphere by having pitched ours into hell. That's what I imagined, although I never shared that with the cops.

When Alan first heard the bit about the mental current strength calculations, he said, "Horse shit," although he glanced at me first, and I suspected he'd said it for my benefit. I guess I don't know for sure what my friends really think of Brian.

It was Adrienne's father who bailed me out in the end. Despite the fact that I'd not visited her parents since returning from the tragedy, except one nearly wordless encounter when I picked up my children, he proactively requested a special meeting with the FBI, at which he described Adrienne's and my courtship, my love for her and for our children, and my great happiness in the family man role. He stressed my voluntary cutting back of my competition travel and accentuated my relative inexperience as a yachtsman. He portrayed me as someone still unknowingly depressed by the loss of my own parents and confused about how that left things between my adopted brother and myself. I surmised all this because the cops ran most of it by me in one form or another to see if they could push any buttons, and then finally closed their inquiry and cut me loose to begin the grieving in private. I was secretly grateful to him for making those intrusions end, although I don't believe I ever thanked him.

I took a leave of absence from Sonnenwende when I got back; my head was in no place to be able to concentrate. Nothing made sense, and I needed to spend every waking hour—and sleeping too—with my two little ones. Needed to make them feel that they weren't anything like alone. We'd line up dominoes together, or play with what little girls think of as action figures, which are invariably stuffed doggies and bunnies and Disney Princess dolls, and wiggle with the hula hoop, and go to the park for a little while if it was sunny, to make snowmen and such. We'd bake cookies, such as I knew how, watch cartoons, and draw. I tried to do the kinds of things I thought moms might do, although I was just guessing. I kept them out of pre-school and kindergarten for two months doing these things, and then ramped up slowly with a half-day of school, with me dropping them off, volunteering twice a week at recess, and picking them up at twelve thirty. After another month we went to full days, because I thought they were as tired of me as they were missing their mom. They re-engaged with their little friends quickly enough, and I went back to busying myself shoveling snow or doing yard work in the winter drizzle, and counting the hours until it was time to go wait in the car in the pick-up line.

I think the kids handled it better than I did; maybe it was because they didn't grasp the concept fully. I couldn't stop my right hand from shaking, for one thing. No idea why. And I had dreams, but really couldn't remember them; I just know I'd wake up sweating, and angry, and ashamed.

I bought the kids a little Beagle puppy, thinking it would help, but the thing got itself hit by a car out in front of the house and I had to plant it secretly out at the farm and then make up a story. I got a terrarium then, with a reclusive salamander, which worked out a little better because nobody gets overly attached to those things...and because it spent nearly all its time under the same brown leaf, so it would be hard to notice if it expired.

Sometimes we'd take little trips, just the three of us, but never to a lake—never near any water, for that matter. We went to the community swimming pool once, briefly, but I wouldn't let them past the ankle-deep infant area. I found myself driving very slowly and acting like a mother hen about everything from sun screen to lunch to bedtime schedules.

Aimless as I was, time had a way of slipping by. The leave of absence was supposed to last a couple of months, but it stretched on for over two years. Hard to imagine even now how that kind of time could just evaporate, with nothing to show for it. I'd always been a guy who did things. Now, I was...I don't know.

I was my dad.

During that grey limbo period, one worthwhile thing that did begin to happen was that I slowly began to see things patching up between myself and Adrienne's parents. I have no doubt that they were in shock for a good portion of that time themselves, but they were made of stronger stuff than am I, and little by little they must have pulled each other out of it. The power of teamwork, I guess. I still couldn't bring myself to do anything like have Sunday dinners over there or anything like that...even though they'd float the invitation now and again, after a year or so had gone by. Still couldn't really even look them in the eye. I know they'd come to the conclusion that my children were all they had left of their own daughter. And they wanted to move on, and do right by her, honor her, take care of her little ones for her. The kids were their second—their last—chance. They knew it, and little by little they started to come back into our world.

So it came to where Adrienne's mother would come by with some little snack she'd made for the kids, or I'd sometimes drop them off over there for a little while on a Saturday afternoon, which was a welcome diversion for all. The girls had missed their grandparents too, I realized, and for their sake we all faked that we had nothing but appreciation and love for each other. We faked being normal; we faked not being broken to pieces. We tried to dance around the edges of emotional repair.

Then later still, sometimes the kids spent the night over there. When that happened, as often as not I'd go back home and sit in the kitchen...stare at nothing...and see memories of a face I missed, and one I despised. I'd recall the promise Adrienne had begged from me on the bow of the boat that last dawn, about doing my best to reconcile with Brian...and I'd tell myself that I'd not been able to give that promise because of who and what he was. Accident aside, because of that ass I wasn't even able to grant her last request. She'd slipped from this world knowing she was dying, I imagined, and knowing she was leaving behind a family that couldn't—wouldn't—unite. I'd sent my wife to her grave denying her the one thing she'd ever asked me to give. I couldn't lie to her. I blamed him for that.

And I wanted revenge.

Bob and Marc stopped by the house once. They commented that everyone was doing alright. True to the obsessive mentality that extreme sports competitors are made of, they could talk about little else besides flying and competing. Lunfer was back into it, too, apparently, and doing well; everyone said that suddenly he was the one to beat. Clearly my buddies had hoped I'd gotten past any ill will, and thought a little chit-chat about familiar things would do me good. But I sat like a catatonic until they made their awkward goodbyes and left.

At some point the money began to run out; I'd already put Adrienne's life insurance benefits into accounts for the kids' education, setting it all up so that I couldn't touch any of it. I didn't want to see a single penny, first of all, and in retrospect it probably helped that I did that, in the minds of the authorities and insurers. I hadn't thought of it at the time, but it probably did help.

I tried not to dwell on the fact that both of my dad's sons had now managed to be investigated for homicide.

Anyway, like I said, the funds were starting to get tight. I'd collected a little disability myself for some of those months, but that had been spent, and unless I wanted to add further tumult to the lives of the kids by losing the house, it became clear that it was time to think about going back to work. I spoke with a counselor a couple of times too, who said she'd been hoping to hear that kind of thing from me. And about that time, Sonnenwende found themselves losing dominance in the pod market, and pinged me to come in and "kick a few ideas around." They were very gracious, but a company must also be practical; what they really wanted was to know if I was ready for full-steam re-engagement, or whether they should sign someone else.

I'd avoided thinking about any such thing up to that point, but subconsciously something must have been going on inside my head for a long time. They offered me a deal where I could design, or compete, or both, and I surprised myself by opting for the full two-course plate. Yes, I wanted back in. I'd been a four-time world champion, for chrissake! I'd scored more points than the next three guys combined since the day they'd started keeping score, and had dominated the World Meets to boot. I wanted all that back, wanted to make a comeback—to rocket right back to untouchable status. I wanted to annihilate Lunfer in the world where I imagined he'd usurped my throne and made himself king.

I began to practice secretly. You can't do it alone, so the word got out, and at some point Adrienne's parents got wind of it. They were not amused. Antoine was no fool, and must have realized the turmoil inside my head, and so he countered by offering to go into business with me. He trotted out this idea of designing and marketing home safety features—must have thought he could leverage my fear for my kids to pull me into a line of work that wouldn't cost them their last parent. He's a class act—they're both class acts.

His proposition even had decent financial merit, but he wasn't privy to my other, darker, more destructive need. I found excuses to delay the business discussions until he realized I was a fish that didn't really want the worm. It's a shame, because it was a good idea, and right at this moment I wish I'd taken him up on it.

CHAPTER FIFTEEN

I started this whole recording by saying that it may be the last telling of my story...and it will be. It's the first, and no question now but that it's going to be the last.

Alone...it's so very deep here. Enveloped by the ocean—my world, my nemesis. Deathly still. I'm going to pop the hatch soon, when I'm done telling the tale.

Alone. For a few moments today I wasn't.

Death. It's not that I fear it. It's that I know it. It has skulked around all my life, brazenly, not even bothering to duck behind a shadow or wear a disguise. I don't fear it. I do have obligations though. And guilt.

When I got back into Deep Flying after the loss of Adrienne, my teammates weren't sure I was ready. They kept dropping hints about maybe doing design and test flight work for awhile. Ease back into the blood and guts part, they advised. They'd never voiced such sentiments before. And they looked at me like you'd look at a stranger. Had I changed that much? I talked less...I knew that. I focused more. They acted like they weren't convinced my focus was in perspective, or constructive.

That was their problem. I'd even caught one of them—I won't say who into the mic—talking with Brian on the phone, at the office. I'm sure it was him. I checked the comp logs immediately, and Sonnenwende wasn't sponsoring the guy or anything...it sounded more like a brief social call, and I didn't know or care which end of the line had initiated it. It smacked of betrayal either way, and I vowed to trust no one.

A year after I returned, I felt ready for a big meet. That was the Outer Banks Open, this past spring, and I've already told you how it went. Sonnenwende suggested afterward that I'd "perhaps rushed things a little," and asked me to step down from competing awhile longer. "Be strategic," they said. I knew they questioned both my judgment over following Lunfer into the kelp and my insistence that he'd planned that whole deadly series of events. They even brought in some so-called "safe team building expert" to give us all a pep talk presentation, during which they went overboard making the point that denying our mistakes is what gets us killed another day. They all but pointed directly at me, going on and on about owning our blunders, facing our limitations, critically evaluating our judgment and motives...over and over and over. I knew all that, of course; they weren't talking to an amateur. I'd written the book on all of that, and I didn't need the likes of them to stand there and tell me I was in a dangerous frame of mind. I could handle myself—I was Nolan Farragut! It was under control.

When pressed, I simply reminded everyone that I was right, that Lunfer would do anything to beat me, risk be damned, and that I wasn't going to let that happen. Mindset of champions, I called it.

Adrienne's parents never knew what really happened at the Outer Banks. None of my friends would have told them, and if they'd known, they'd never have agreed to watch the kids for me for other meets...for this one right now, the Chilean Worlds. I didn't even tell them how I'd placed in the Outer Banks, which was poorly after zeroing that day. I simply said I needed one more good win to ice the whole thing this year, and I hinted that if I did it, I'd retire and let this be my swan song.

In truth, I couldn't win the World Championship this year even if no one else had come today. I didn't fly enough meets, and the Outer Banks was a complete dud. Mathematically, there are a dozen guys I can't catch, points-wise...and Lunfer is one of them. I don't have the numbers. My buddies know it, too, but they've said nothing.

I came anyway. It would still have been the statement of the century to wade in here after being just a name on a wall of plaques for some years, after doing nothing more than get stuck on kelp and nearly killed this season...after all the whispers that I'm washed up, that I've lost my nerve, that the sport has outgrown this old dinosaur...to come in here and still blow them all away. Annual point totals would turn into who-cares trivia—nothing but back page sidebar notes—but I would become immortal. If I could just win the World Meet, right here, right now, before I hung 'em up...I felt I'd still make it clear that no one could ever touch my legacy.

I realize now that I wasn't thinking about my kids. Not about Sonnenwende either—they still thought I was flying for their name, but I knew I'd turned that page already in my mind. Last page, last daring drive, and I'd take it beyond limits that would make other men quake.

Normally you can't fly the Worlds without some minimum meet participation and point total on the year. But being a four-time World Champion, I'm grandfathered in. I didn't care that they all thought of this as a back door, a celeb pass, an honorary deferment. As long as I could fly with the best of them, I could shut them up. I'd done well enough in the earlier tasks and heats this week, staying in the hunt, although not quite leading. Maybe a little conservative, but I was biding my time. I'd finished low— sixteenth—on the second day, but made up for it on Day Four by diving under Helmut Van Der Voor seven seconds before the line, spoiling his hydro-efficiency by passing an inch from his hull, and taking third...a patented move of mine that few have ever figured out. He never saw me coming.

And today was going to be the big day. I stood on the tug this morning, noting only a thin layer of very high clouds, and sensed that the convection was already working; I could see it. I could smell the start of the upwelling of cooler water from the ocean bottom. Some of the water movement was thermic, and some came from the convergence of an offshore surface current with the warmer water of the continental shelf. As I leaned over the rail and regarded the playing field of the week's final task, I shook off forebodings, trying to stay centered.

We were anchored pretty much where the meet officials had been towing from on the previous days, and with the average bottom well over a hundred feet down it was more than deep enough for that. I'd had no hand in designing the courses for this comp; they do their best to maintain separation between the staff and the top competitors in a World Meet. That was okay with me, because I'd designed and influenced so many race heats I knew how teams of officials thought. And I was waiting for one particular kind of task to be called—the one in which I'd prove my dominance.

The other Sonnenwende guys were doing alright, too; in a way it felt a little bit like the good old days. I realized I wasn't the only one who'd been in a disconnected state the last few years. The guys had been hurting too. I'd pulled them all together in the first place, after all—I was their first real mentor—and it must have seemed to them like the heyday was gone, there for awhile. But I was back now, as intent as a person could be, and that kind of mental heat...mental precision...has a way of feeling like excitement, and of rubbing off on everyone else. Bob and Paul were having the best meet of their lives, I believe, finishing in the top two dozen

almost every day. Alan and Marc had done that
before, but this week was no exception. Will had
cut his usual place finishes by half. They were all
high on the experience of the week.

I was a handful of points out of first, with ten
other guys, over a two hundred point spread. A
few naysayers were already marveling, but I
knew they'd seen nothing yet.

It was still really early. The others were only
starting to rise and shower, or were sipping
coffee in the makeshift on-board tug café. Things
were just beginning to stir.

I caught the barest sound of shuffling...and I
made the mistake of turning to look.

He was there, maybe fifteen feet behind me—
trying to decide, I guess, whether to boldly slap
me on the back or slink away before I saw him. I
said nothing, didn't smile, didn't frown, didn't
nod. I raised my eyebrows as if to say that now
was his moment to state what he wanted, and to
be quick.

Brian had gotten quite good at Deep Flying in
the time I'd been off. I'd lost track of time, but
the span of months was considerable, and he
really had no other world of friends, so he'd
flown. True, things had also changed for him in
this crowd, as they had for me—we were both
poison to talk to now. His role in the loss of

Adrienne was a question mark in everyone's mind that had smoldered and festered over time. My role too. They'd all heard about the investigations, and nobody wanted to dredge it all up by asking me outright, given that I'd kinda lost my way for a few years after it happened...but it was what I'd call an "open" secret that I blamed Lunfer. So they all kept their distance in general. I was pitied, and he, with his bully-like mannerisms and the irresponsible tilt of his head, was half-suspected, and given a wider berth than before.

Someone tried to tell me he came back to the sport because he was lonely and was hoping to reunite with me, but I was in no frame of mind to listen to such crap. He knew where I lived. No, hell no, he wasn't welcome there, but it's stupid to think that I could take a shotgun to him from my doorstep but would go hug the guy if I bumped into him at a meet by accident. I told them if he wanted to run into me then he had a death wish.

He'd gotten good. His well known affiliation with me, and the fact that he'd continued to win meets in his bathtub of a pod, landed him a berth with CrocRiver, the biggest Australian gear maker, an outfit that I don't think had even existed when I was at the height of my comp career. Evidently they wanted someone stationed in the Northern Hemisphere anyway, to make appearances and such, and so Lunfer became a rep for them. I still don't think he could string six words together to make a sentence, even counting drool and middle fingers, but it seemed his flying was speaking for him. Some time after he destroyed his own pod beaching it at the Outer Banks, which I'd always assumed was because he'd just had an impulse to go drink himself into a stupor, he found these sponsors, who got him into their pro line, which for added safety was built around the new Life Chamber technology—a machined metal chamber in his case, or so I assumed, which was heavy but strong. What with the strange, almost spooky affinity he seemed to have for vector math, suddenly he was winning bigger meets. Suddenly he was their finest horse.

I'd never placed any stock in the "Lunfer the math whiz" rumors; or if I did, I'd thought of it as autism. Maybe it was related. I do know that vector calculus is at the very heart of handling all kinds of soaring craft. If he had some kind of natural ability, it would account for his meteoric rise to stardom in this sport. It's happened before in soaring aviation. I hadn't given him credit for his amazing shallow water feats in the Outer Banks, but I knew he'd dusted me good. I told myself that my territory was deep. But he'd become an "in yo face" force of nature in the Deep Flying world...my world...and right now, in this World Meet, he was one of three guys tied for first. So he was actually ahead of me. Besides that, he had one of the top point totals for the year...as compared to my nothing. This lumbering idiot, this crass, reckless bully who lived for beer and stole from kids back in school and who'd spent his teens in a juvenile prison, was poised on the verge of capturing the World Championship in this niche, high profile sport.

I thought that's what he'd come to rub in my face now, as he stood well back from me, hands in his pockets, shuffling. But I kept looking at him, begging him to start his brag, waiting for the obscene strut, knowing how sweet it was going to be when I knocked him off that high perch—when I obliterated his chance for the title and became the most inspirational story the sport had ever seen.

We stood there. Two full minutes passed. Finally he spoke.

"Doooooooode."

Imagine traveling twice the length of a continent to deliver that message, I thought. He couldn't even pronounce it right.

I gave it another minute before replying, "Very well said, Brian. Now if you'll excuse me, I'm planning my flight." I wanted to get rid of him, and I wanted him to know that whatever happened later in the day was all by design.

I turned back toward the sea. Heard nothing more. Eventually I could make out that the meet organizers were having a discussion at the edge of the café area, and I moved in that direction, sliding off to the side along the rail, noticing that Brian had already left.

The World Meet committee had selected this place because of the extreme clarity and depth. The ocean off the coast of Antofagasta, Chile— and where we were, which was between there and Tocopilla—has some seriously deep sections. There are also a few protected bays. The stretches in between are ideal for Deep Flying. The land is as dry as anything you can possibly imagine, which makes for very little runoff and adds to overall water clarity. On some parts of this coast, there has been no rain in living memory. Forests are exotic pictures in a book; timbers are the perfectly preserved things that Europeans brought long ago to shore up mines in the mountains. Antofagasta is a major city, as the word major is defined down here, and offers sufficient lodging and eating options that a major event can be held without thoroughly disrupting the inhabitants' lives. Hotels both modern and classic are easy to find, as is fresh seafood. The city welcomed the Worlds, and it seemed that most competitors were happy to go experience such a singular place.

I cared about none of that; wasn't here for culture. I'd spent the months leading up to it studying charts of the ocean floor, and I found what I wanted. It was down there. I knew where.

At nine on the nose, people began to stumble out of the café area and out of their bunk rooms. Small launches came alongside, bringing those competitors who'd elected to berth in hotels on shore...or who had been forced to because they'd stayed out too late and had missed the last meet shuttle an hour after midnight. They scrambled now onto the main deck of the tug, over by the bridge, all jostling for a good view of the course map, the weather summary and radio buoy coordinates boards, and places where they could hear the loudspeaker better. Last day. Pilot's meeting.

I took a position on the edge of the mob. I told you before, I knew how these meet officials think, and I was pretty sure I knew what task they were going to call. Up to now we'd flown two long, straight, high-mileage timed race-to-goal tasks, two north-then-south-then-north zigzag turn point tasks, and one day that lapped us twice around a big course oval. They love to mix 'em up, to separate the men from the boys, and there was really only one kind of task left unflown.

The Meet Head spit air into the microphone a bunch of times to test that it was working, until it got annoying. Finally she resorted to actual words. "Last day, people," she reminded us, stating the obvious. "It will be decided today. We hope you've enjoyed the World Meet here on the beautiful coast of Chile."

Applause, as anyone would expect.

"We have a bit of a photo finish going on this week..." she blurted then, her voice booming to the point that they had to turn down the amp. She glanced at the leader board and waited until the grinning and back-thumping had subsided. "We've gotta find a way to spread the scores a little...look at these dozen pilots here." She swept her hand across the top section of the chart, where I and the other front-runners were listed.

Now I had no doubt. She was trying to make a case for stretching us all along the coastline.

"And in particular, we need to separate these three!" It was Charles Crouse of the UK, the Brasiliero Joao Coriali, and Brian.

Get to the point, I was thinking. Just say it.

And finally she did. "The task committee has decided to go a bit free-form on this closing day of the meet. Give you all a chance to make your own decisions. See what you can do."

An audible wave of soft murmurs propagated, front to back, from the throats of those who still didn't know where she was headed.

"So...no specific goal today. The direction is up to you. Furthest from the launch tug wins the day. No out-and-returns, no doglegs, no cross-current stuff...unless of course you want to wrestle with all that."

Chuckles.

"Read the conditions and get what you can. For this final task we call: Open Distance!"

It took half an instant, and then it sunk into their heads. They cheered their lungs off as I walked smugly away. I'd known, of course, and had been ready for weeks. Interesting that it was all going to go down on the very last day, though. Delicious.

The others no doubt thought it would be an easy task—no time pressure, except what the conditions of the day forced upon us. No real rules, either—no need to prove we made a turn point, no pylon cameras to flash our hull number in front of. Hell, they were all exaggerating right about now, we can go straight out to sea and try to make it to...Hawaii if we want to! Or maybe blow right by Hilo on our way to Guam! Just pick a direction, make turns as the conditions we encounter change that choice, and try to go farther than anyone else.

And basically they were right. The concept was rather simple. Of course the honor system prevailed in an Open Distance task, to some small degree—competitors were expected to turn on their transponders and radio in when they surfaced, so that the end of their flight could be pinpointed and their distance measured. It didn't matter that much, because once you're bobbing away on top, you can't go very far by wind and waves...not compared to the speeds you can make gliding below, anyway. And it would be blind luck to pop to the top and discover that the breeze is exactly in line with the direction that would stretch your score. I guess it's possible that a competitor whose meet placement is neck-and-neck with another pilot could change the result by drifting a little extra before radioing in, but they draw a half-kilometer circle around your call-in position and consider all points within it the same, so there's some slop. It's not as precise as timing a race to a goal line, where they can measure a tenth of a second if they need to, but it's close enough. Mostly they rely on the fact that the pilots will get hungry and thirsty out there, and call in.

And it wasn't gonna matter, from my perspective. We readied our gear. I went and put my damp, clammy wetsuit on, thinking about my most likely first moves and listening to hear who was planning to tow down first. That part was key, because I didn't want anyone else spotting me and leeching off the decisions I made.

My pod had been too wrecked to salvage after the Outer Banks. I'd recovered it to get the instrumentation inside. Some of that had been ruined by salt water, when the thing had rolled on its way to the surface, tumbling corrosion across everything bolted to a bulkhead while its busted wooden rib was skewering my leg. I sold a lot of that stuff to people who thought they could clean it up and get it working...or maybe because they wanted a piece of history—the hand-made electrical wiring harness that failed in the famous Nolan Farragut pod; the subsonic transceiver that Nolan Farragut had not been able to use when he was almost eaten by a shark.

Sonnenwende reluctantly loaned me a pod to bring down here. I say reluctantly because they weren't convinced I was ready for an extreme big-water meet. They knew I had the skills, and knowledge to spare, but they still had doubts about my judgment, my state of mind. They also knew the first thing I was going to do with any pod they "loaned" me was to modify the hell out of it, which meant cut it up, and most likely turn it into a one-meet contraption that nobody else later would be suicidal enough to fly.

But they could hardly refuse to enable the father of the sport to enter the World Meet for his big comeback attempt in his last year. Pilots would have told that scandal for the rest of their days. So they gave me a choice of a nice machined rigid thing and an older model, slightly dented with some exposed top rigging, hoping I had the sense to pick the newer, safer capsule.

It goes without saying that I did what...what you'd expect me to do—I picked the other one. I gutted it completely, working in their shop in the dead of night, mostly to avoid questions. I knew what I was doing. I basically stole an egg-shaped modular carbon fiber Life Chamber out of a showroom pod, though, and forced it into the aqua-glider I was altering. Actually what pissed them off was that I took one of the new chambers made of multi-walled carbon fiber nanotube material, cross-linked by irradiation. Unbelievably expensive—they'd made a handful of them for Navy oceanographers. The stuff was transversely aligned in the lay-up to take advantage of its incredible tensile strength, and protected against plastic deformation with titanium micro-column inserts and special epoxies. They say the molecular bonds are stronger than any diamond, and I was counting on that.

This stiffened up the cockpit in a serious way—everything is compressible to some degree, as I've said, but theoretically, combined with a special breathable gas mixing system, a re-breather, and the new Bodner unit—a small, slick little high-speed centrifuge thing powered by a fuel cell that actually extracted a bit of dissolved oxygen out of the water—altogether the new technology multiplied the depth I could go to by around eight, maybe more, as compared to an open water diver. A pilot in a pod outfitted like this could flirt with much deeper water before dealing with the whole toxic oxygen level thing. And I further braced the chamber with a couple of—metal this time, the hell with wood—pillars, hoping to make it even more rigid. Because of all that added weight, I had to put back some buoyancy in order to meet the minimum. I stuffed neoprene in between the Life Chamber cockpit's wall and the outer hull rather than the usual semi-stiff foam, to occupy that space with something other than water. It would give me the float force I needed for approval to fly in the meet.

What was more, the outer skin, made of the older alloy—remember I'd chosen the battered old-generation hull—was more flexible. At depth, that neoprene I'd stuffed in was going to compress, and my buoyancy would then decrease. Like I explained before, it was going to give me a slightly better glide ratio. It would cut my top gliding speed too, but I knew my flight plan would more than make up for that.

I expected the resulting contraption to be able to withstand depths I'd never been to before. I trusted that it would all work out; I trusted that I'd return home to my kids. I only had to fly it once in serious pressures, I told myself.

Two more innovations they'd come up with while I'd been away from the sport were better, more reliable pressure controllers...and I was counting on that...and the advent of the kick plate. The kick plate was not something everyone had, or even wanted. Cork class gliders, which would not be here at the Worlds in more than token numbers, never came near enough to the bottom to ever use the things. A kick plate allows you to depress a pedal in the cockpit and mechanically cause a levered surface to extend out the bottom of your glider. In flight, it acts like a spoiler, to reduce glide efficiency when you need to rise up over obstructions. Also a side benefit is that if you get too near a reef, you can put your foot down on it and use it to fend off impact from your underside hull. The outside panel looks like one of those slanted oil pan shields under a car engine, except that you can deploy it and let it recede at will. Good to plane overtop masses of seaweed and such, too. Anyway, I added one, just in case; it deployed only about five inches below the pod's undersurface, but that seemed like enough.

I decided I'd tow down late—let the other Unlimited and Formula class pilots, who were lumped together as one big group today, get down there ahead of me. I wasn't going to need much convection anyway, and I wanted them out of my way. I went back to the rail and watched the other guys vaulting over with rebel yells, landing with a splash twenty-odd feet below, then swimming out to where the pods were tethered in a long string behind the tug. One by one they unclipped their gliders, which fanned out like so many flatfish escaping from a stringer and covering the surface on either side. A large silent splash caught my attention far to my right, toward the bow end of the rail, and I realized it was Brian. First time I'd ever seen him not hamming it up with a bunch of admirers. Like I said, poison; a loner now...like me. I'd noticed earlier that someone had changed the spelling of his name on the pilot board from "Brian" to "Brain," and it had made me chortle to think he'd become the butt of such thinly veiled mockery.

He swam under my position now without looking up and continued on, out to the pods. Still a strong swimmer. I watched to see if he was going to pull that "snorkeling" trick as an excuse to check out my gear, but he gave it a wide berth and continued on to the end, where he was met by some other members of the CrocRiver team.

What was he flying now? From that long distance it looked different somehow. Still a big thing—well, it had to fit around him, after all—but it looked like it had been altered. If so, it must have been a last minute deal, because I'd seen a photo of him winning a regional meet three weeks ago, and the pod shape had been different. Or maybe they'd switched it on him. This one looked less spherical, more feathered on the sides...and maybe of later vintage. The glint of some new composite? Didn't quite look stock, either. I wondered how much it would flex at depth. I wasn't worried for his safety, I just noted that it looked different.

Funny...I'm telling this now like I told all the rest of the stories—like I've thought about it forever. And yet...this stuff just happened this morning. All the little things I remember...and each of them, in retrospect, had an effect on what has happened today. All the seemingly insignificant things...they add up...the random stuff, who said what, who failed to notice what, who felt this or that in their heart. And here I am, now, at the end. Waiting to pop my hatch.

At the rail this morning...the loudspeaker crackled back to life. "Eleven o'clock! Line forms here!" The tow winch operator was yelling from his own mic now—from aft. Pilots who'd not gone over the side yet were donning wetsuit hoods and jumping in. The haphazard flotilla of aqua-gliders already free of their tethers was forming into a long line, each pilot hanging onto his own rig and the stinger of the pod in front of him, in the order of who wanted to be towed down before whom. There were as many theories on what would be best as there were pilots—some thought that getting down there first would give them an edge; others—like me—wanted the field cleared out before they went under. Still others didn't know which would be best, and split the difference, putting themselves somewhere in the middle, which to me meant they'd reap no advantages at all. Good-natured splashing marked team boundaries everywhere, and I spotted my own mates about to gang up on the Canadians while their backs were turned. That was a move that obviously lacked forethought. I decided it was time, took a deep breath, and vaulted the rail. I was feeling good, convinced I'd win the World Meet today, and swam out to save my boys from drowning at the hands of former hockey players.

None of my team had originally intended to fly this comp. It was expensive, what with the travel and all, and they were not all sold on cold, clear, deep water. I reminded them that that could make for strong convection, but some of them were family men too, and the prospect of braving hypothermia, serious rips, and the possibility of getting lost in a part of the world where they couldn't speak the language did come up. My voice was that we'd do it together one more time. Then I'd retire, I said, leaving the throne wide open for them to wrestle over, myself sticking to pleasure-soaring at vacation resorts.

The massacre was over by the time I got to them; they'd paid the price in Pacific water up their noses. I chuckled and swam on, reached my pod, and took the short bow tether in my teeth, towing the thing off to the side. With its abused nose cone and outdated top rigging, it looked obsolete by two years. No matter; I'd been able to pilot it into the top dozen up to now, and the pod's relatively ancient heritage wouldn't matter from here on out. I'd bridge the technology gap with personal magic.

Everyone knew the standard drill by heart: Tow down to some workable depth, release, try to get lower, and then stay down and go. If you can, always hug the deepest holes as you go your distance, where the least mixing takes place. If possible, do your entire flight hopping from deep section to deep section, from workable sink to workable sink. Despite the minimum buoyancy requirements in each class, there were still subtle float force differences, pod to pod, so rise rates were always going to vary. Every pilot would have to seek out sink for himself or herself...some more than others. Since any depth lost means more sink has to be found, keeping low and trying to stay the hell away from upwelling water was the extent of the usual flight plan. Turning buoyancy into forward glide is the pod's job—what these craft are born to do. The pilot's job is to use the range it gives you to find more downwelling, and then stretch that continual "go down, go forward, go down, go forward" strategy for miles.

Everyone kept it sane, though, this quest for depth. Only an imbecile would forget that death always watched with an open mouth from below.

A French pilot was grabbing the big iron hook and attaching it to his pod's release. I looked on from some distance as he reached back into his pod...probably adjusting the breathing mixture to his regulator or turning on his comm circuits...then wedged thick neoprene legs into thigh straps, sealed the hatch over his head, and through the small, clear front window gave the thumbs-down. The winch operator set the spool to "payout," the tug's voice roared, and Jean Pierre disappeared, leading edge first, into the depths. The final rodeo had begun.

Other pilots followed, each in turn. The tow queue remained orderly. I watched while a few tried to delay, messing with hatch doors too much or asking questions to which they already knew the answer, perhaps thinking that every minute helped them, assuming better conditions would occur later as the day warmed. Everybody's a closet meteorologist. Sometimes guys drag their feet to help their teammates, too—they get their best pilots down there and then others on the team slow down the line—like bicyclists tying up the pack. I wasn't sure what the thinking was today, but there were a few launch potatoes in the crowd...until one competitor called 'dunk,' and everyone in front of him had to either tow down without delay or else exit the line and re-enter at the back. I was glad of that rule now; I wanted them all to get out of my way and be gone.

All week, the front-runners had been getting deep and staying deep, hopping from sink to sink as they raced to each successive turn point. There would be a few collisions in the mayhem and impossible visibility—paint is always traded—and those with more strategic control would win out until the gaggle spread out. I've always believed that if you're deep you can avoid these frenzies, shooting out ahead before the school forms in the thermal below the first marker buoy.

But I now realized that today was going to be different, and not just because of the Open Distance task. In contrast to the previous days, the high clouds I'd spotted at first light had just barely begun to evaporate; the sun was getting brighter. Someone of lesser experience might reason that this would impart more heat through the clear surface water to the depths, and increase the convection, like sunshine increases atmospheric instability for soaring pilots in air. But I knew a bright day would shut things down here. It would cause a serious plankton bloom, clouding the surface water, drastically cutting the light that penetrates to deeper levels. The thermal strength today would actually become weaker as the hours went by. Other than a little convection fuelled by some tiny geothermal vent here or there, I now reckoned bottom of sink would rise to no deeper than a hundred fifty meters, despite the high hopes and the forecast. All this was even better than I'd dreamed. I had to get down there before it was all gone, but other than that, the others would be counting on finding sink all day. And while they were scratching their heads and struggling, I would divert boldly from the tried-and-true when the time was right.

I called to my teammates, who were well ahead of me in the tow line, wishing them luck.

"What's your flight plan?" Alan asked across the water. "Where do you plan to head?" His emphasis on direction meant he assumed the standard "go down, go forward" see-saw. I cupped one ear and tilted my head to fake waterlogged hearing, not wanting to shout out my intentions to flirt with the jaws of hell.

See...there's a strangely named trench about sixty miles offshore here, and only a couple dozen miles from our tow point. A smaller tributary of the famed Peru-Chilean Atacama, even this little brother canyon is so deep it has never been explored with anything more than sonar. In places, it's around four miles to the bottom, as it descends in a southwesterly direction into the larger one, which is deeper yet by a full mile or more. I reasoned that the water has got to be very cold down in there, and probably little mixing occurs. But I spent months leading up to this meet studying similar topography in other parts of the world—places much shallower but shaped the same geologically—places that have been explored. And they all tend to share certain aspects of how the water moves. Also, at two thousand feet and more, the rim of this gouge in the ocean's floor is not exactly shallow, but there are still a few wrecks that have settled on and around it over the centuries. I studied reports of some of those, and the later recovery of artifacts from them, much further south, by salvage hunters. And so along the near rim of this ultra-deep rift, I believed there was a current, flowing just back from the edge but parallel to the depths. The convergence of marine mammals on the canyon's side every summer also told me it had to be there, bringing krill and other edibles.

I wasn't able to estimate the velocity of this current except to guess...likely not quite as fast as an aqua-glider's top glide speed...so one might think I'd be wise to ignore my theory in favor of a conventional flight plan. But at least that current was sure to move, and never stop. I'd never have to pause to work sink. And now, if the convection was really going to degrade, then the rest of these fools would be struggling all day, scratching for tiny little gains in depth. It would turn into a duration contest, where the best scratchers and the least float-loaded and those with the flattest glide ratios would just barely prevail. And then, when they were all safely back on the tug—even my own teammates—downing cold ones and lamenting the results and trading tall tales of the high saves they'd almost made, I'd surface beyond the far horizon and radio in my coordinates, to smear all the glory on my own face and claim both the cup and my place in history.

So there was no point in second-guessing now; I'd already decided. If I could get down to it, I would fly the ragged edge of Abismo Del Diablo—the Devil's Trench.

One by one we were towed down, and suddenly it was my turn. I paddled into position as the tug came around, adjusting my comm headset and checking the valves on my breathing mixture tanks while it swung its stern toward me. They tossed me the cable as I sat atop my pod, and I hooked it to my release. Then I checked my pressure system, climbed inside, and sealed the hatch. Through the cloudy window I looked at the tug guy and "gave him the thumb," as we say, then quickly got into position. The big engine's noise erupted, transmitting through water and hull. I felt the old familiar lurch, and the world went from bright to filtered blue beneath a pile of frothy foam. I kept her straight and let myself plane downward. As the cable payed out, putting distance and depth between me and the tug, it got quiet, and serious.

CHAPTER SIXTEEN

I pinned off at the prescribed thirty-meter max depth threshold, and hooked a thermal right away. Sink-detect variometer chirping, I cored it to a little sless than sixty five meters—just over two hundred feet—before the thermal sink column shattered against a weak inversion. I'd expected that, of course; you never get an uninterrupted progression of warmer to colder as you keep going down. Alternating between my sustainable forty-up float rate and an occasional burst of lift alarm, I snooped out another stronger downwelling and took it much lower as I drifted it north-northwest.

That's not where I wanted to get to...but I was committing a little subterfuge, you see. Most of the others would be starting in that direction, I knew, before they began to spread out more westerly, dreaming of hilariously glorious, impossibly huge distances, of passing Maui to starboard followed by the Johnston and Bikar Atolls...while actually getting their tiny little forty and fifty milers. I could see their ghostings on my screen, sweeping in big, silent, grey brush strokes from right to left, or vice versa. Several times thermaling pilots came so close I could make out their hull colors with my naked eyes. One or two of them might have been able to see mine.

We were still in a big gaggle, maybe a couple dozen pods, all told, sharing this wide downwelling core with each other. It was the first really deep water just west of the tug, and the first and best sink everyone had found right off of launch. Those who'd towed early had no doubt moved on by now, but those who'd come down around the time I had, or who had made mistakes and lost depth, were here with me, all stacked up at various depths but all working the same big core. There are rules of the road about circling direction and right of way, but no one ever pays much attention. Their focus is on winning more than on being fair. It's not like hang gliding, where a collision becomes instantly deadly; here, you can damage another pilot's linkage and at worst get yourself disqualified, but only if it's witnessed...and damaged pods usually float out. So it gets to be the wild west down in these gaggles.

When I reached about eight hundred fifty feet, still well within the pressure capability of my Life Chamber, I cranked a hard diving left, peeled back under the school of other pods, and left the sink. No one would notice; they'd simply think I'd bobbed out of it and was going off to snoop for another, somewhere in the gloom. And we were nearing the depth below which even the most daring pilots never chose to fly, so already the crowd had thinned to next to nothing. Whoever was left, and I couldn't tell and didn't care, would be bearing west on a glide about now anyway.

I spread my pod's nose angle a little to max out my aspect ratio. It makes the thing less pitch stable, meaning the nose will lift and drop in hair-trigger response to my pitch inputs, but there would be so little convection down here that I didn't care. The new setting was going to improve my glide, and that's what I wanted. Consulting my directional screen, I dimmed everything down, then executed another shallow bank and headed southwest, into a cloudier zone that surrounded the big blue-water thermal I'd just left. Once masked from view, I worked to depth again in a weaker thermal, now unseen by anyone. From this point on, I knew, I'd be electronically untrackable.

It took another six weak thermals and more than two hours to get down to where I wanted. I was making for the hypothetical current on the edge of the trench. I figured I might begin to feel the water movement at around thirteen hundred feet, but when I got there it was very weak. I managed to stumble onto a well defined seam between drifting water and still, and used that to do some dynamic soaring, cutting back and forth across the invisible eddy line in ever increasing speeds, in a tight oval pattern. I don't know of any other aqua-glider pilot who can do it—who has ever done it or ever mentioned it, anyway—but then almost none of them came out of the world of flying in air. I used the technique to boost my speed as much as possible and then pointed nose-down and dove it all out, trading energy for depth.

This whole plan was clearly going to be no picnic; I'd have to earn it—I'd have to use these kinds of unheard-of skills to make it work. That was okay; if I pulled it off, this feat would stand forever. I was at fifteen hundred feet, and the drift was a bit stronger, as shown by my increasingly southward position.

There was real danger here, I knew. This route, and the notion of riding such a current, was unknown. If a strong river of water did exist on the Abismo Del Diablo's eastward edge, there was nothing that prevented it from swinging out over the deep black without warning. Once there, with no sea floor below it, a pilot could drop below the current and enter the still, frigid water of the trench itself, through which little convection ever moved. Compressed below neutral buoyancy, a craft could descend into the void and disappear forever.

But I intended to stay back from the lip somewhat, counting on my screen to show me where that edge was, and bottom turbulence to keep me off the dirt. I expected the current would provide light up-pressure here and there where it rolled over obstructions, like a creek does when it piles up in front of a rounded rock. I'd use that so-called bottom rotor as a kind of cushion from the terrain. I just had to make sure I never followed the current over the edge; if it tried to take me there, my plan was just to let myself float up and away from it. Had to stay alert.

Noting that the drift was strengthening, I kept my glide as flat as I could and swung my direction north for a moment, into the oncoming, then abruptly pitched down and dove through the flow...and got an extra sixty feet of depth, not far off the bottom. It did the trick; I crossed from kid stuff into the seriously powerful, lateral, laminar surge that I'd postulated had to be there. It was sure and strong, and I found myself suddenly part of it, knifing silently over extremely old rocks and layered dust, a grain of flotsam in a mighty ocean's palm. I had been right! It was here. I was going to do a two hundred mile day.

I had entered what's known as the Mesopelagic stratus—sometimes called the Twilight Zone or the Lifeless Zone—where at one time was thought no life existed. There's little if any light, first of all, and so plant life is virtually zilch, and so they reasoned there must be no food as a result. In turns out that about a fifth of the bio-material the ocean creates finds its way down here, slowly filtering from above like sediment in a bottle of Port. A naturalist named Forbes, sailing in the Mediterranean on a British ship in 1841, called this the Abyssal Zone. He tried, but found no life at all. Of course part of the problem back then was that there was no way of dredging stuff up from this deep. I mean, think about it—a rope long enough to extend behind a ship and drag a net through water that far down would have to be incredibly strong...not to mention so long that from the ship, the net itself would be literally beyond the rearward horizon—beyond the curvature of the earth. Even as recently as the Second World War, when they first began the frequent use of sonar, it was a shock to discover what existed at these depths—

the ocean floor they'd measured at a thousand to fifteen hundred feet during the day would suddenly rise up to be much more shallow on moonless nights. Turned out their signals were rebounding from millions of organisms, zooplankton and fish, that would migrate upward from this zone in late evening to feed on plant material. They'd come up when they could handle the light level, and when predators couldn't see them as easily, and then descend again to these depths at first light. Sonar operators called it a "false sea floor" because the signals were telling them that the depth at night was a fraction of what it had been the day before.

They say there are a lot of things that live down here, although for animals big enough to see, the density per cubic mile of water is still probably negligible. What creatures there are have adaptations that allow them to hunt, to hide, and to mate. Bioluminescence—the ability to glow—lets them blend with the light filtering down from above when their enemies are below them. Swim bladders are present only on the fish that ascend at night; the others just sit on the bottom their entire lives. No fan coral or other stuff we typically picture when we imagine the sea floor, either. Fish sizes are small overall—a couple of centimeters to a couple of inches, mostly—because food is always scarce. Big eyes are common, like wide aperture camera lenses, for drinking in what visibility there may be. There are optimizations for focusing up and down while sacrificing the side-to-side...color filters on the eyes, to more readily know the difference between light from above and light given off by another fish...strong bone structures...bizarre shapes.

I couldn't see any of it, of course, since there was essentially no light at all, by human standards anyway. And I didn't want to risk burning battery power to run with outside illumination. I tried to shine a flashlight out the forward window once or twice, enough to convince myself that terrain below was flat and mostly devoid of relief, save a small lump here or there. I saw no huge Colossal Squid eyes looking in through the portal, no razor-jawed lantern fish dangling glowing baubles for me to reach for. I saw a deathly still seascape of nondescript settled dust stretching into the gloom.

Flying without seeing outside is beyond any kind of aviation or deep sea soaring I've ever done. I'm accustomed to using instruments as a second opinion, not my only source of truth. Powered aircraft pilots do it all the time—they call it IFR for "Instrument Flight Rules"—but in hang gliding we always said that acronym meant "I Follow Roads." Piloting solely by instruments is fine if you have a whole network of FAA guys and sectional maps and other resources to assure you there's no mountain directly ahead, but it's a little different buried below untold tons of water half a mile below the next closest human being in a place called the Lifeless Zone.

I made my peace with it by use of the flashlight, until I was convinced nothing out there was going to change. Clearly it hadn't changed in many millions of years. I'd continue to conserve power, and continue to pursue glory. I began to fly mostly by feel, sensing the uplift that signaled I was nearing the crest of the rolling bottom rotor, and then sensing the lull that followed.

Becoming part of the flow is intensely therapeutic. Kayakers and fly fishermen and surfers have said so forever. Even watching a gurgling stream, even listening to it, calms the mind. There was a serenity about it now, so incredibly deep, so incredibly silent—and yet here I was. An entire planet of billions upon billions of organisms up above, and only a couple of arrow worms and microbes had any impression of my movements. This zone was a huge, liquid crypt. I stopped being overt in controlling the glider and began to just ride. That was the point, right? Just let it take me, with the great power of silent distance that it had.

So I started to drift near stall speed, letting the current do the work. I "porpoised" along, sometimes slightly raising the nose when the roil off the bottom pushed up just a little, sometimes relaxing the pitch control completely and resuming a more level glide posture. Staying what I estimated was twenty or thirty feet from terrain, I settled into a predictable, easy rhythm. I was able to maintain my general proximity to the ocean floor, where the current appeared strongest. My flight computer indicated my ground speed at an amazing twenty or more miles per hour, on average. I felt I could maintain this drift for eight hours, maybe longer; it didn't matter to me whether I surfaced after dark. I'd get my two hundred, all told...and on a day when that would be four times what the number two guy would pull off. How would that be for a statement from a dinosaur?

An hour later I was still savoring that single thought. Imagine winning by so much, and doing it while...while reading a newspaper! That's what I'd tell them I'd done. Their jaws would hit the deck as they pictured that. The quote would make the evening news in front of a billion viewers, and I'd transcend the aqua-gliding world. Screw them all; I invented this sport, and I owned it. I'd land product endorsements...roll out a Farragut Wing of truly superior design, as had always been my plan...a line of Farragut wetsuits, crossing over from niche sport gear to mainstream. Might be on Sports Illustrated's cover...maybe get a cameo in the Swimsuit Issue...take some of the models for a flight. Never return the calls of whoever had looked at me with pity. Feel like a god for the rest of my days.

Two hours into it, my technique still seemed almost trivial. Must have gone farther since I entered the main flow than what anyone else would get for their entire flight. What with the distance I'd gone just to find the current, this meant I'd already won the day and the World Meet. Again. Well, let's just run up the score, put it into the realm of the untouchable, I thought. Swan song.

So I rode...I rode the ocean's breath.

I knew I was still descending, although very slowly; the current was following the rim of the Abismo Del Diablo down, down, in its bid to join the even deeper mother of all trenches, the Atacama, a hundred miles offshore. As long as I was in the current, I told myself, I could control things. I checked the depth meter for the thousanth time; pressure had ramped up steadily for the last forty minutes. I was approaching two thousand one hundred feet! Should I float a little higher...accept a slower current speed? Might add a margin of safety, although I wouldn't go as far if I did. Hey, don't lose your nerve here, don't overreact, I thought; don't spook. There was no major creaking, no bolts shooting across the cockpit, like in old crippled sub movies. Stay the course, the hull was handling it.

I knew how much work the others were going through right now. Many had already floated out, kicking themselves, or consoling each other back on the tug, with hotdogs and brews in hand. Some of the front-runners would be among them; others would still be scratching for all they were worth, feeling blind-sided by the way such a hopeful last day had so suddenly shut down, pleading with the cosmos to make sure everyone else was having the same dismal time of it. They'd squeak out that extra mile, praying it would be enough, which it wouldn't. I thought of Lunfer struggling out in front of the rest—I knew his shallow water skills would serve him well today, although they'd be so outclassed by my deep magic he'd probably quit the sport! I imagined him searching and grimacing, wheeling and cutting, all the while straining for a glimpse of me on his screen as he worked like a dog to keep ahead. I laughed. Many thought he was now the best pilot around; they thought the sport had left old-school mentalities behind. Brian

Lunfer, Swaggering Math Whiz Wonder Boy, best that's ever been, finally the sport has caught up to where his genius is revealed...and today I would beat him so badly the magazine would misspell his name.

I was still laughing when I was thrown heavily against the instrument panel.

"What the hell?!" I think I said aloud, righting myself and checking quickly to make sure I'd not snapped off any of the control levers. They're not designed to take being pounded by the weight of a grown man...nor, I noticed, is a rib cage designed for it either. But I had bigger things to worry about. Sudden impact is not something one expects during flight of any kind, and it's never good news. I dragged myself over to the window and peered out, shining the little flashlight forward and down. My pod was sitting on the bottom! Stopped dead. It was tilted at an odd angle against something. Cripes, I thought, I've flown myself into the goddamn bottom! I quickly scanned every corner of the pod's interior, in a panic lest I discover even a drop of seeping water. Thankfully I saw none as yet.

Okay, so what had happened? I hadn't been paying attention to my heading, pitch, and water speed. Could I have hit kelp? No, stupid question, I reminded myself, but that's what the brain does when under sudden severe stress—it goes to what it knows. Okay, calm down. What, then? Hit an undersea hill? I saw no evidence of thirty-foot-high terrain in front or out to the sides. What, then? Maybe I'd stalled, drifting along down-current as I had been; I guess I could have done that...in fact I'd been flying almost at stall for some hours. I supposed that the bottom roil had failed to support me, or had rotored me somehow below the current's laminar flow. But then...why hadn't I simply floated up out of the current? Why wasn't I rising gracefully right now? That's the fundamental safety valve of these things, right? You float?

I must be hooked on something...stuck on something under me, I decided. Whatever the reason, I was dead in the water, and on the other side of the hull it was very dark, and very deep.

This was not good. Aha, the kick plate! Just the sort of thing I'd installed it for. I tried it, and got it to partially deploy, but it did nothing. I appeared to be hung up on more than just the edge of a rock, or a bit of sand. Cursing, I tried the kick plate again, more aggressively, but only succeeded in raising the craft a little off the bottom, from where it settled back. At least I was a bit more level now...although that wasn't necessarily a good thing. I thought maybe the kick plate might have more to push against from this new posture, but it didn't seem to make a big difference in several more attempts.

You jump a foot in the air when you're so incredibly alone and then hear a noise; I smacked my head against the aluminum mount of one of the reinforcing pillars I'd installed, because my hydrophone speaker had crackled to life.

"Dooooooooooooooode." It was Lunfer's voice.

At first I thought he was transmitting from onboard the tug, and I reached up to switch off the unit; the last thing I needed was that voice as the final thing I'd ever hear. I had my finger on the switch when the doubt hit me; it wasn't garbled near enough.

"What the hell are you doing on the comm link?" I demanded. ...I'll try to recount how this whole conversation went.

"It's da Meet channel," he said. True enough, and it meant he was still in his pod.

"Well?" I replied, "something you want? I'm a little busy, so go back to the tug and get another beer. I'll be along after a bit."

He didn't answer, although I heard him momentarily key the mic. And it sounded almost like someone spat, like tobacco. I could imagine what the floor of his pod must look like.

I tried the kick plate again, but only settled back to the bottom. What the hell...?

Brian's mic keyed again. "Need ta get you up outa that," he said.

Huh? "Where the hell are you, Lunfer?" I demanded. "Are you still flying? Still out on course? Because I am, and I'm going gangbusters." Did he know I wasn't in motion? How could he know?

"Yer on course, I'm on course," he replied.

"Where?"

"Both of us is nowhere, I think."

"Where are you Brian?!" I was getting impatient. And I wanted him to think I was too busy flying to be chatting on the radio.

He waited for a moment, as if there was something he was reluctant to admit, and finally said, "Need ta get you outa that dirt."

"You know where I am? You can see me?"

"I can see yer pod out a corner o' my glass."

How on earth could the guy be here? It wasn't possible. I'd sneaked off low into zero visibility, had become a grey piece of nothing in a grey ocean, had dived into a current no one else knew existed, had flown it for hours...and yet I knew that he did know where I was, and that he was out there. His was not a signal transmitted from the far-off tug and converted to sound waves by a comm buoy half a mile above me; I wouldn't even hear him—our short, recessed antennas weren't that sensitive for receive. He was near.

And while receiving signals all the way from the tug wouldn't be possible, transmit was another thing; the hydrophones were optimized for safety—for getting signals out. The World Meet officials were probably listening.

There was no more need for subterfuge, and so I decided to play this for all the drama it held. "So you followed me, Brian. We're at...looks like almost two thousand three hundred feet, on the rim of the abyss. We're probably a hundred fifteen miles or so out. And you followed me. What the hell does a guy need to do to get some privacy?" I imagined the chuckle that would bring, up top.

But I was taking this seriously. I mean...the guy had followed me...at least, I certainly hadn't followed him. For that matter, I'd proven at the Outer Banks that I wasn't up to the task. How had I not known he was there? How could he keep me in sight? Maybe the dim red light on the tip of my stinger, and a little glow of my instrument panel coming out the bow window...and maybe he'd spotted my occasional use of the flashlight...although it hadn't been very frequent. Did he guess my flight plan? At any rate, the guy was good, I had to admit.

"Dooooooode." It now sounded like he'd switched from hand-held mic to voice-triggered...like we do when we need our hands on the controls.

"What?"

"Let's git outa this jam."

"Who's this 'we'?" I asked impatiently. "I'm doing fine. I can fly my own glider. Go fly yours, Brian. Give me some room. Where are you, anyway? You don't show up." I slapped the side of my screen.

"About fifteen...uh...yards behind ya," he replied.

"Well, make it fifteen hundred," I said, and stomped with renewed vigor on my kick plate. "This is my idea and I'm gonna make it work. If you're so good, go fly your own flight."

There was silence for a long time. I waited, but heard nothing. Couldn't get a glimpse of him in any direction out my window; the flashlight wasn't going to reach fifteen yards anyway in that gloom, and I assumed that he'd already overflown my position since saying that. I tried to change the angle of my pod by manipulating the kick plate, but it always settled back in about the same place. Where was he? He'd said behind me...but I could see nothing there, overtop, or anywhere.

I went back to assuming I was alone—that he'd called from somewhere above and then flown on. I stomped the kick plate a bunch of times. I couldn't figure out what I might be caught on, but I knew if I couldn't solve it, I'd eventually run out of air. It was all looking more like the watery grave impression that had hit me earlier.

I sat there for a long, long time. Maybe twenty minutes. Couldn't figure out what to do.

But then I heard his voice again. "Dooooode," he repeated, making maximum use of his large vocabulary. But I also thought he sounded a little insistent this time. "Fergit the meet. Let's just git you outa here."

"Lunfer," I shot back, "I said go. Don't tell me what to do. You wanted to beat me so bad you followed me. So go. Do it. Win. I don't need you to get out of here." The retort was a slip-up, an admission that I had a problem. I was annoyed because it was all coming apart at once—my victory, my revenge. He'd clearly caught the current too, and he'd now go on and win. I couldn't even shake the guy in my moment of defeat.

"Would ya...let me help ya? There any problem wid dat?" Playing the radio drama himself now, I muttered.

"Yes, there's a problem with that," I returned, finally losing it completely. "I can't stand you. That's the problem. Neither can anyone else! You think they admire you, but they're laughing at you, dooooooooode. They always were!" It was cruel. That was the state of mind I was in.

"Wh...why? What you want from me? Why you sayin' dat?"

"You disgraced our family! My mother, who tried to give you a chance! What a fuck-up, stealing, and all the fights, flunking everything in sight...and you killed my Dad, you fuck!" I'd never said that to him before.

He was silent for a minute, and then in a faltering voice he said, "Dad...Dad, uh, died...while I wuz gone! I never...uh...."

"You killed him, Brian, you might as well have shot him full of blood clots with a needle! You broke him down, and shamed him, and he died. Was it worth it? Was murder, and the drugs, and that cheap trailer trash tramp, all worth it?"

Silence.

"You tried to get me killed in the Outer Banks! Left me there to die! Wanted the Deep Flying crown, I guess?"

"I called...when I figgered out that...."

Wait...what? Was he suggesting...? How, for that matter, did those two fishermen happen to be there dragging a piece of water with a hook, for a guy in a type of watercraft they'd never heard of in their lives? I never actually knew who'd called them or flagged them down, or why people like the local sheriff had been looking for me. And the tug had gotten a muffled radio call, they said. Did Brian beach his pod, destroying it on the rocks, to...was that what he was trying to say so eloquently now?

I would have given it more than a half-moment's thought, but my hate went far deeper than small questions about telephone calls and kelp. I'd lost everything, you see, all my life, and now very possibly my children, although that was yet to sink in. But I was venting it all, at this point, in a foul, bitter rage, all the resentment from all the years. And there was no going back. He didn't even deserve to be confronted with Adrienne. In my mind, even talking about her to him polluted her memory. But I couldn't stop myself.

"And my wife. Where is my wife, Brian? Huh? Take a glance out your window right now. Do you maybe see her stripped bones drifting by? I think the current is just about right here, don't you think? I think she might take just about three years to get this far...." I choked up and had to stop, unsure if the gagging of my words was wrath or the remnants of despair.

I composed myself just enough to continue, wanting to stab him again and again with the jagged shard of hatred. "I mean...Brian...she's dead. A corpse. Never found. You stopped us from looking for her—for Adrienne, Brian, for my wife! And because of that she drowned. Her children will never see their mother again. Won't even remember her face. You idiot! You reckless, stupid moron! I mean...what were you doing in the water that day, Brian?!"

The guy was crying. I could hear it. I could hear muffled sobs.

Unable to hold back my own tears now, I slowed my voice and repeated the question one last time. "What were you doing in the water, Brian?"

"...I wuz...uh...lookin'."

The image that entered my mind froze my blood. Looking? Could this guy, this judgment-challenged moron, have been...trying, in some unbelievably stupid way...to help? Could he have felt my instant implication of blame and deliberately tossed his own carcass overboard, dooming himself to probable death, and all to...flail around in that freezing, treacherous water, thinking he might figure out which way the current would take a body, "looking" for Adrienne? I remembered saying that I could have forgiven stupidity.

I couldn't handle the alternate interpretation...not after all the years and all the pain. "You know what, Lunfer?" I replied, changing the subject. "Just...forget it. Forget I brought it up. You asked me what I want from you, and I'll tell you." I gave it a moment so there'd be no mistaking. "Distance," I said. Then, "Yeah. That's what I want. Open distance. That's what the day called for. So...all the best, have a nice life...and now beat it."

I almost shut off my radio...but was sure there was no need. I didn't bother to reach way over and hit the switch. He'd get the message, he'd fly on.

I must have wasted another quarter hour of air doing nothing. I was confused in a way I'd not been for a long time. Hate has a way of keeping things in the focus it endorses, and I'd been so sure, for so many years. Maybe I was faltering because of the stress of being stuck on the sea floor, of the mighty ocean holding me by my Achilles with its malevolent, unseen hand. Maybe the oxygen was getting a little thin. Maybe my hatred from all the years had finally run to the limit of its reach. I know that every bit of so-called evidence I carried in my heart, every major piece of my painful history, was suddenly more in doubt, more blurred, than it had ever been.

I sat. I wiped my eyes. I tried the kick plate again, but although I could jostle the glider, she wouldn't rise. I needed to get clear of the emotional crap...to relax, to think. What was I caught on? There seemed to be enough motion; my buoyancy should have jerked me free by now. Could I have punctured the skin, the hull, or gotten a rock caught on the undersurface, like in the kick plate's hinge? I'd never heard of such a thing before.

The radio...but very softly now: "Kin I help you get outa here?"

"Why the hell are you still there?"

"Kin I please...."

"No," I said to the question he hadn't finished, and checked my breathing mixture gauge. Why had he followed me today?

I didn't need him. What I needed was to get out of here! Okay, small breaths; calm down. Checked the air mixture gauges again; I had about thirty minutes left in the green. I thought about the troubled look my wife's mother had let me glimpse when I'd left their house last week;

same look she'd had before the sailing trip. I spoke my little daughters' names aloud, reminding myself of why I must not panic.

At this point I knew Lunfer still hadn't gone. There was some agenda, or some reason. He was conserving his breathing mixture, like I needed to do. Eventually he spoke, and his voice had the quality of someone who's made a watershed decision.

"Well, damn you, I'm still gonna get you out."

"Why the hell are you still here? ...And how is it you're not floating out, anyway?"

"Mebbe I got a wingtip hooked under an old coral stump."

There's no coral here, so he was lying. Or...was it just sloppy communication, and he'd snagged himself on a rock? On purpose? Was the guy that good? I'd never heard of anyone with that kind of control. I tried to shut that out and concentrate.

Lunfer, the oaf, the grinning fool, took charge then, demonstrating a decisive quality I'd never before seen in him. "Gotta act now, dude. I'll tell ya the truth...I think we both already too low...got no float left."

Why I hadn't realized it I'll never know. But he had to be right. No hooked wingtip; he was just sitting on the bottom, like I was. Waiting to die. That's why I couldn't float free—my pod, the neoprene layer of my pod, the layer I'd designed to be compressible so that I could secretly get an increase in glide, was so compacted that my displacement could no longer overcome my weight. Both our pods were too compressed to float anymore. An irrecoverable position—once we'd stopped moving, it was all over. And Lunfer had known it...and still he'd come in, still he'd landed, and sat there, watching and waiting for me. Why didn't he try to kick off?

"Sun's dippin' low up top," he added as an afterthought.

"Why did you follow me today?"

"You know...yer my bro."

So there it was. While I was bent on robbing the world title from him, he was busy being...my bodyguard? He'd followed me all my life, fighting in school because someone mouthed off to me...and the quarries, when I'd so resented having to be saved by my younger sibling...and Deep Flying. I heard someone say once that the best Guardian Angel is the unrecognizable one, the one who doesn't look like the paintings in church.

He'd mentioned the sun dipping low; I wanted to see another one of those. "Why didn't you go up and get help, you ass?" I hollered in my standard, useless voice of blame.

"Ain't nobody up there could even find dis place. Be pitch dark on top in another hour...couldn't a'got there an' found my way back. Even if I could, while I wuz doin' it, you'd of been suckin' yer tank dry."

"So you landed."

"Same pickle as you now," he said, "like ol' times." He gave a heavy sigh. "Ain't no horsemen comin', either, dude. We gotta surface on our own."

"I can't move, and neither can you, Lunf...Brian. You're flat in the mud."

"I'm still up-current of you, dude. Reason I landed here. Mebbe I kin pop up a bit by really stompin' my kick plate...drift toward ya. Try to give you a thump. Mebbe jar ya loose."

"And then what?! We'll both sink right back down...or into the trench."

"Not if we try now, before things shut down fer good. Gotta be some weak mixin' still goin' on, somewhere. We can use that to git back up."

"You mean...work LIFT?!"

"Why not?"

"I've never done that before!"

"Sure ya have, doooooode," he said dryly, "you bobbed out before...and I know you never do nuthin' by accident." It was a reversal of the old joke about hang glider pilots who land short of goal and claim to have accidentally mounted their instrumentation upside down, only to spend the day working sink instead of lift. I was doomed to die with a comedian.

"But...what if we don't find any upwelling?" I asked.

"Yer a pilot, ain't you? A pilot gets the job done."

I thought about that as I coiled to jam the kick plate. I could hear his voice-activated mic keying as he jostled and grunted to escape the mud suck. By the sound of it, he might put his big foot right through his hull.

I knew every team up top would be listening to all this; they'd have heard what was going on and would have called a meet-wide gathering. Except for our voices coming out of the speaker, you'd be able to hear a pin drop on the tug deck.

"Drifting a bit now," Brian said, after a huge grunt and thud. Then, "Okay, here I come." Such cool understatement, for our one and only shot at survival.

He piled into me from the side, stalled, out of control, the momentum of his big, heavy glider transferring to my sleeker craft. I timed my stomp and kicked for all I was worth, and together the two jolts broke me free, to drift for a moment like he was, with the current. I'd popped about thirty feet off the bottom, which meant I had that much to work with, to find some lift. Thirty feet, staggeringly low odds, one-shot deal. I knew my glide ratio was optimized to work against buoyancy, not gravity, and I tried to estimate and hold an angle of attack that might give me greatest range for the thirty feet I had to spend. I didn't know for sure what that inverted glide slope would be down here, but thirty feet probably gave me, at best, a seven-hundred-foot run in any one direction...with whatever random heading I chose determining whether I lived or died.

I didn't know how to decide...I hesitated...I faltered. And in that instant...an image flashed strangely into my mind...or could have been in the window, I don't even know...spooky...wet hair draped across, and one eye looking at me over the crest of a floating log. I'm not saying it was an apparition—I'm not saying anything—but I whispered her name, and I turned toward the place I thought I'd seen her...and ran my one shot out, max of seven hundred, straight line, and prayed. At six hundred twenty feet out, over a mound of rock so ancient it had crumbled to dust before ever glimpsing a living thing, I found the thread of lift that would save my life.

"Wish I was up there wishin' I was down here," I muttered, hands shaking on the controls for fear of blowing it. Ever so gently I stayed in that whisper of rising water and worked a very flat circle into a hair more clearance off the bottom. And then, trembling, began another. It took eleven full turns, but by some miracle that soft sigh of lift more than two thousand feet down held together. Twelve circles; thirteen. I'd gained enough to dare look down through the window, to find that I was now about seventy feet off the dirt. Still dire as hell. I worked it to ninety, then a little more. This just might happen, I almost thought.

The core got stronger at its very center and I took a big chance and cranked a steep, sharp three-sixty, standing the glider on its wingtip as I tightened the circle. And it held! I accelerated upward.

"Yee Haw!" I hollered, mostly to myself, having momentarily forgotten about Lunfer. "I hooked one! If my gauges are right, I might be at neutral buoyancy in another hundred feet!"

"Awright..." Lunfer's voice said through the speaker. "Work it, dude...work it." He didn't sound right.

"Where are you, Brian? What's happening?"

"Didn't get the jolt you got, bro. Not much...range...ta work with."

"What? Where are you? Are you stuck now?"

"No...I...still tryin' to find lift...." He was speaking like someone who's afraid to take a good deep breath...like somebody who has dived off the lip of the abyss in a last prayer to find an impossible boomer from the depths.

"Lunfer, don't do it, there's nothing but cold and more pressure down there!" I hollered. "You're compressing more with each foot you lose...that thing will crumple like a candy bar wrapper! Get out of there!"

"Too late," he said. "Walls are steep. No place even to land. I'll...find somethin'."

"There's NOTHING!"

"Ever been down here?" He was whispering now.

"How deep are you right now?"

"Lost another two hunnert I think...mebbe."

"Lunf, plaster that thing into the wall now! Brian, I'm coming back down after you."

"No! You ain't doin' that, bro. Not a damn thing you kin do but get in the way, get yer ass lost at sea. I'll find somethin'. Always do. Must be a lower transverse current somewheres...mebbe I kin use it like inverse ridge sink, against the angle o' the walls...mebbe further down."

"How much breathing mixture you got left?"

"Less from all this talkin'. Gonna sign off now fer...awhile. I'll surface somewhere an' call you." He was silent for a moment, then added, "Nolan...I'm sorry about Adr...about her."

That was all. I was back into positive buoyancy, and now began to work sink to stay as low as I could, listening, calling for him now and then, asking for his status. At considerable risk of going right back onto the mud, I regained the current and flew it for at least four more miles along the trench rim, this time watching how close I was to stall, my eyes glued to the screen for murky images of Lunfer's craft. I called repeatedly, ignoring my sagging oxygen needle and the difficulty I was having drawing each succeeding breath. I begged him to respond and report his position, encouraged him to stay conscious and keep looking at his vario. But I never heard him transmit again.

When my oxygen tank was down to the gas in the hose itself, I leaned out the mixture and switched to the emergency reserve, trying to remember when I'd last recharged it and hoping there was still something left in that small canister. And I ran that past its rated limit too.

Then in reluctant defeat I found a small band of ridge lift, rode it upward into positive buoyancy, and let myself rise, choking, until at last the surface broke over my pod's cowling.

I haven't popped the hatch yet, although the pressure equalizer now says I can. I know when I drink in the cool night air it will taste like shame.

CHAPTER SEVENTEEN

I'll never again tell this story; it's my confession of hate, and death, and blindness, and loss. Once I pop the hatch, the tale is over. I guess the battery went the distance after all.

Sitting here, alone. Sea is calm, pretending it's not our enemy. So deep here...right down there, directly below me. If there's a current up here I don't want to know about it; I don't want to know where Adrienne's bones swept off to, or my brother's.

I cut the radio. Transponder's on though. When the tug homes in on it, and finds me, they'll haul me out, give me hot soup, welcome me back...but I don't yearn for it, for the reunions, except for the one with my children, and to reunite with the memory of my parents, and my wife. Right now I just want to float. Alone.

They're going to try to hand me the trophy for the meet. I don't want it. My sport...mine...but I give it to them. It's Kipling's pretty dagger with the jeweled handle, and death's shadow is always upon it. This was my last comp, and my last flight.

Deep Flying has been my life. A creature I sired, it has seduced me with adrenalin and fame, has given me purpose, and direction...and a framework for hate. A hypnotic thing. It epitomizes Life itself, in a way—we launch into an unknown...a deep, silent, savagely indifferent space...and we ply the currents, choose our course, selfishly go as far as we can...try not to float out. It's all solitary; the gaggle of compatriots is an illusion, a beguiling ghosting on the screen. A fool's daydream...whether we spend our lives professing private closeness, or displaying open animosity—open distance. And we all run out of depth in the end; we all hit the barrier. If we force someone else into it first, so that we might go on flying, well, that's the game, isn't it? And we chuckle and think no one need ever know.

Maybe it doesn't matter so much who breaks the surface first.

They'll never find him. It'll make headlines. People not in the sport will use it to prove that nobody should ever fly or dive or...maybe they're right. The pilots will disparage him in his absence, behind my back so I don't feed them their own teeth. They'll say he was strange anyway, a loner at heart...the mannerisms of a retard and the manners of a bully...just like high school. They'll dredge up nonsense like...somebody remembers him once saying it would be a hoot to live in South America...anything they think of that sounds revealing...a whole lore will spring up. That's how people are. I'd like to think he found that lower transverse current, and that inverse ridge sink. That stuff is vector math, and I'd like to think he made it. I'd like to get a phone call out of the blue one day, from South America.

At some point, when they're old enough, I'll have to give my daughters this recording...tell them the truth. They'll probably ask why I never went to find him. I guess I'll tell them it was because of the distance.

About the Author:

Michael Vorhis was born to a large farm family in Midwestern USA. He has resided in or extensively traveled Australia, New Zealand, Italy, France, Germany and other parts of Europe, the New England states, and Colorado, Wyoming, and other stretches of the Great American West. Most recently he makes his home in Northern California with his wife and daughter. His passions include high alpine mountaineering, the paddling of free-flowing rivers, soaring flight, fly fishing, string instruments, cartooning, baseball, volleyball, the martial arts, photography, the open road...and writing.

He has developed and published fiction and nonfiction, including novels, short stories and screenplays, for more than three decades.

Contact information:

Email:
Freeflight-Publishing@vorhis.com
OpenDistance@vorhis.com
Archangel@vorhis.com

URL:
www.vorhis.com/FreeFlight-Publishing.html

Look for these and other fine works by Michael Vorhis:

ARCHANGEL

(Five-star Suspense Thriller novel; ISBN= 9780983898504; published 2011)

http://www.vorhis.com/FreeFlight-Publishing/Archangel.html

The shame of terrible deeds past can drive a man to self contempt. So it is with Mick Calahan, anonymous, disconsolate, shielding the world from himself in priest's robes. But a disturbing assignment and the desperate trust of a young woman threaten to make him choose between staying buried and unleashing the phantoms that haunt his past.

Drawn into Gabriella's taut, troubled paradise, Mick harbors a dark secret—that his signature quality is not virtue. And the woman knows, and the town will come to see, that their deliverance could compel this mysterious man to oppose evil by becoming it.

ARCHANGEL is a deft marriage of suspense, complexity and compelling beauty through which honor, malevolence, and forbidden love collide. Reviews have spoken of "story-telling genius," taking fiction "from good to great," and a plot that constitutes "a class-five hurricane." It is a taut, thrilling, profoundly memorable experience—a masterful work.

Stick Riders: Of Men whose Keen Wits Miss Naught, and with Glory

(First published in Insider Magazine, Cincinnati, Ohio, 1988)

A larger-than-brains tale of rugged high adventure that lionizes two swashbuckling young explorers—tougher than biker gangers, more clever than sixty two percent of marsupials—as they straddle the unlikeliest of manly machines through the dry and deadly Australian Red Centre.

An American Sporting Man Goes to Hell

A hilarious (sadly also true) tale of gloriously misguided athletic expectations and how they can instantly wither to so much overcooked gnocchi when steeped in a small town Italian soup.

Real Heroics from the Less Than Renowned

(First published in Hang Gliding Magazine, 1997)

The story of a Regional Cross Country Hang Gliding Championship in the high deserts of the American West.

Flying in the Face of the Gods

(First published in Hang Gliding Magazine, 2001)

The story of the first and only World Hang Gliding Slalom/Speed Championships, and the American team that took home the gold.